Hi, I'm JIMMY!
Like me, you probably noticed the world is run by adults.
But ask yourself: Who would do the best job
of making books that *kids* will love?
Yeah. **Kids!**

So that's how the idea of JIMMY books came to life.
We want every JIMMY book to be so good
that when you're finished, you'll say,
"PLEASE GIVE ME ANOTHER BOOK!"

Give this one a try and see if you agree.
(If not, you're probably an adult!)

For exclusives, trailers, and other information, visit jimmypatterson.org.

UNBELIEVABLY BORING BART

BY JAMES PATTERSON
AND DUANE SWIERCZYNSKI

ILLUSTRATED BY
XAVIER BONET

JIMMY PATTERSON BOOKS
LITTLE, BROWN AND COMPANY
NEW YORK BOSTON LONDON

Copyright © 2018 by James Patterson
Illustrations by Xavier Bonet

Hachette Book Group supports the right to free expression and the value of copyright. The purpose of copyright is to encourage writers and artists to produce the creative works that enrich our culture.

The scanning, uploading, and distribution of this book without permission is a theft of the author's intellectual property. If you would like permission to use material from the book (other than for review purposes), please contact permissions@hbgusa.com. Thank you for your support of the author's rights.

JIMMY Patterson Books / Little, Brown and Company
Hachette Book Group
1290 Avenue of the Americas, New York, NY 10104
JimmyPatterson.org

First Edition: September 2018

JIMMY Patterson Books is an imprint of Little, Brown and Company, a division of Hachette Book Group, Inc. The Little, Brown name and logo are trademarks of Hachette Book Group, Inc. The JIMMY Patterson Books® name and logo are trademarks of JBP Business, LLC.

The publisher is not responsible for websites (or their content) that are not owned by the publisher.

The Hachette Speakers Bureau provides a wide range of authors for speaking events. To find out more, go to hachettespeakersbureau.com or call (866) 376-6591.

Names: Patterson, James, 1947- author. | Swierczynski, Duane, author.
Title: Unbelievably Boring Bart / James Patterson, Duane Swierczynski.
Description: First edition. | New York; Boston: JIMMY Patterson Books®
Little, Brown and Company, 2018. | Summary: Brainy twelve-year-old Bart attracts little attention at his new middle school near Hollywood, California, but whenever he can get around his gym-coach father, he secretly hunts electricity-guzzling aliens.
Identifiers: LCCN 2017035235| ISBN 978-0-316-41153-0 (hardcover) | ISBN 0316411531 (hardcover)
Subjects: | CYAC: Middle schools—Fiction. | Schools—Fiction. | Family life—California—Fiction. | Extraterrestrial beings—Fiction. | Video games—Fiction. | California—Fiction.
Classification: LCC PZ7.P27653 Unb 2018 | DDC [Fic]—dc23
LC record available at https://lccn.loc.gov/2017035235

10 9 8 7 6 5 4 3 2 1

LSC-H

Printed in the United States of America

*For my extremely (not) boring
children, Parker and Evie.*
—D.S.

PROLOGUE

THE BIG SLEEP

So I'm standing in front of my social studies class, and I've just started giving the most important report of my life. I'm nervous, because a *massive* part of my grade depends on this.

I'm about three sentences in when I realize: *Houston, we have a problem!* I look up from my paper and quickly scan the classroom.

"Er, as I was saying . . ."

You know how you look out into the class

and hope for a bit of encouragement to keep you going? Maybe a smile? Or at the very least, some eye contact?

"Umm . . ."

But there's nothing. No reaction whatso-ever.

That's because *everyone in the classroom is asleep*.

Or maybe they're all actually *dead?* It's kind of hard to tell.

What the heck is going on here?

In the movie version of my life, you'd hear crickets chirping. But I'm pretty sure I've put the entire insect kingdom to sleep, too.

That's right. The reaction in this classroom proves it:

I am the most boring middle schooler in the universe.

But wait!

Don't stop reading!

I promise, there's more to my story than you think, and it's totally and completely *not* boring. My story involves bizarre creatures, last-minute escapes, daring computer hacks, double crosses, and even the threat of total global destruction.

But who am I? And how do I know all of this?

The only way you'll find out is if you keep reading.

BARTHOLO-WHO?

My name is Bartholomew Bean, and I wasn't always the most boring middle schooler in the universe.

In fact, I fit in pretty well back in my hometown of Philadelphia. Sure, you had your usual gang of overachievers and super-jocks, and more than a few knuckleheads and bullies.

But most of us were somewhere in the middle. You know, *ordinary kids*. It was easy to blend in when a whole bunch of us were trying to do the same thing. In Philly, you never wanted to stand out because that's pretty much painting a target on your back.

WELCOME TO RANCHO VERDUGO, CALIFORNIA

"WE HOPE YOU LIKE THE SUN, BECAUSE, BOY, WE'VE GOT PLENTY OF IT!"

Then a few months ago, my dad got a new job and moved us to a city 2,700 miles away called Rancho Verdugo, California.

The second part of the name comes from the mountain range that's in our backyard (the Verdugos), and the town's first name comes from . . . I honestly don't know. Because it rhymes with Verdugo? Because everyone here used to be cowboys?

Anyway, Rancho Verdugo is right next door to Los Angeles. You know, LA. The City of Angels. The place that always gets blown up in all those disaster movies.

"You're going to love it, buddy," my dad told me. "The weather's absolutely insane! It's pretty much sunny outside all the time."

"I hear the weather's really nice in Hawaii, too."

"Oh, please. Rancho Verdugo is so much better than Hawaii. Just wait until you see it."

"Do people in grass skirts bring you pineapple smoothies in Rancho Verdugo?"

"Bart, you're going to have to trust me."

And I did. I trusted Dad right up until that crazy-hot summer day we pulled into town. Soon I realized my dad's idea of "nice weather" was a blazing death ray beaming down onto the top of your head at all times.

"Seriously, Dad? It's like a billion degrees here!"

"They say it's a little warmer here in the summer. But it sure beats Philly, doesn't it?"

Clearly, my dad loved the sensation of being a bug on the sidewalk while someone held a giant magnifying glass over him. Maybe he relished the sound of his own body sizzling as he slowly turned *well done.*

But do you want to know the real problem with Rancho Verdugo?

It's super-close to Hollywood.

LA-LA LAND

I know what you're thinking:

Hollywood? Man, that sounds so lit!

Yeah, no. It's pretty darn far from lit.

Because Rancho Verdugo is so close (and by close, I mean right over the hill, the same hill with the big white H-O-L-L-Y-W-O-O-D on it) to the Entertainment Capital of the World, people from all over the country flock here to Make It Big.

Which means the halls of my school are jam-packed with some of the *most interesting middle schoolers* in the world.

I mean, look at them!

Right up in front are the YouTubers.

You can tell because they're glued to their phones. All of them have their own shows, watched by people who have *their* own shows, which in turn are watched by other people who have *even more shows*. (Who has time to watch all these shows?)

Anyway . . . see those kids behind them, with the sets of huge headphones strapped to their heads?

Those are the Electronic Musicians. They use their laptops to create "music" that sounds like a smartphone when you put it in the microwave for thirty seconds and then smack it with a hammer.

Farther down the hall you have the Indie Film Actors. They mumble a lot and look at their shoes and pretend they're on camera at all times. Whatever you do, don't step into their scene. They'll yell "CUT!" and have you forcibly ejected.

And waaaaaay back at the end of the hall are the Future Olympians. They run a lot and avoid carbs and sculpt their bodies into machines that are perfect for running a lot and avoiding carbs, I guess.

All of them incredibly cool. All of them hopelessly fascinating.

And then there's me.

By comparison, I'm a total zero.

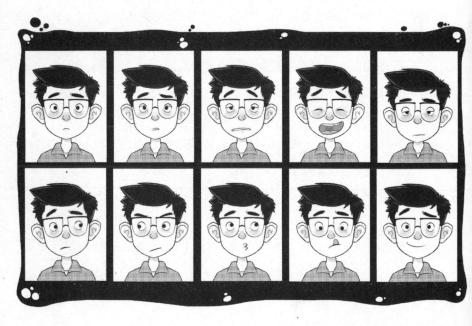

A bore.

Snoozeville. Population: me.

No visible talents.

No clear purpose in life.

No reason to exist, really.

And the problem is. . .this makes me stick out like a sore thumb in a bucket full of fingers!

Okay, that's kind of gross. But you know what I mean.

OH, I'M SORRY, I DIDN'T SEE YOU EXISTING THERE

My typical day starts in homeroom with Mr. Lopez checking attendance. I'm always in my seat on time, ready to get this day going.

Not because I'm excited about school. I just want to get it over with as soon as possible.

Now, Mr. Lopez is a pretty chill guy. He never yells, even when other students are acting like rabid squirrels. He'll just glare at them, and pretty soon they get the idea that they'd better calm down, or else.

But Mr. Lopez is so chill that sometimes—okay, maybe like *half the time*—he forgets to call out my name.

Even though I have perfect attendance, I'm probably marked absent half the time. Which isn't going to make my dad very happy.

Alas, there's no time to stick around to tell Mr. Lopez that I am actually there and not still asleep in my bed or playing an RPG on my laptop or test-piloting experimental aircraft forty thousand miles above the school.

Because when the bell rings, I have approximately 4.3 seconds to transport myself, as well as my school bag (which weighs 847 pounds), to another classroom that is two buildings and three floors away.

My dad always says to give everything my "best try." And I do. Sometimes I even raise my hand in class. But do teachers see me? Nope.

It's like I'm one of those optical illusions where you can't see me unless you stare at me cross-eyed.

Maybe if my teacher stares at me long enough I'll finally appear, like one of those magic sailboats in those goofy pictures at the mall.

Now if I could stay invisible all the time, it wouldn't be so bad. Like I said, back in Philly, I blended in with the rest of the ordinary kids. Which kept me safe.

But because I'm not a YouTuber, or an Electronic Musician, or an Indie Film Actor, or a Future Olympian, I tend to stand out to a particular type of student at Rancho

Verdugo Middle School.

And that would be . . . the *bullies*.

My best guess is that they pick on me because I'm breathing perfectly good oxygen that someone far more interesting could be using.

Or maybe because they're bored. And when you're feeling bored, nothing quite satisfies you like pouncing on someone who's boring, like, *all* the time.

Then again, maybe they pick on me because they think I'm just shy. And if they push me far enough, I'll suddenly snap and do something interesting . . . like bust out some killer kung fu moves!

But I've never even tried to chop a head of lettuce, let alone a human being. What am I saying? At Rancho Verdugo Middle School, most kids would consider a head of lettuce far more interesting than me. (Especially if it's organic, shade-grown, free-trade lettuce.)

Anyway, you'll meet all these bullies soon enough. They're kind of hard to miss. And they have a nasty habit of popping up when you least expec—

Oof!

Um, that would be Giselle, a.k.a. the Golem.

(You know the legend of the Golem, right? Giant statue made of clay, but sprinkle a little magic on it, and the thing comes to life to stomp your enemies into itty-bitty pieces?)

Anyway, Giselle the Golem's got five inches on me, along with about eighty thousand pounds of pure muscle. The Golem's favorite thing in the world is pretending I don't exist.

I'm serious. She plows right into me like the *Titanic* hitting an iceberg—only *I'm* the one that snaps in half and sinks down to the floor. Glug.

The Golem never says "Oops, sorry."

She never even *slows down*.

What's really weird is that even if the Golem is standing across a crowded hallway, she'll target me like a heat-seeking missile. Apparently, she's got some kind of bat-style radar that *pings* whenever I'm within range.

Bully-dar.

The next thing I know, I'm kissing linoleum.

But there's something even worse than playing Tokyo to Giselle's Godzilla.

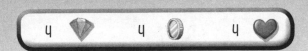

4 💎   4 🪙   4 ❤️

TEACHER'S PEST

Psst. Hey."

There is one kid who pays close attention to me. He's pretty much in all of my classes, and somehow he *always* manages to be sitting *right* behind me. Even when the teacher decides to change things up by moving our seat assignments around, he's there. It's as if he can defy the laws of time and space!

"Yo, Bart!"

I do my best to ignore him, but this only

deepens his resolve to make me turn around. He'll start *flicking* the back of my T-shirt. Not hard enough to sting or anything. But constant enough to drive me out of my mind, like a steady drip from a leaky faucet.

Flick.

Flick.

FLICK.

And then, involuntarily, as if some force has seized control of my brain and nervous system . . . I turn around to face . . .

Nick, a.k.a. the Mimic.

Nick the Mimic looks at me like he's a puppy dog and my face is a giant treat.

"What?" I whisper in the quietest, loudest voice I can manage. Naturally, this happens at just the moment Miss Howard at the front of the classroom stops speaking. And my "WHAT?" sounds as subtle as a drum set shoved down a fire escape.

Miss Howard turns. Gives me a frown. Then goes back to talking about the American Revolution.

"Bart! Guess what?"

Oh, boy. I have no choice but to whisper back: "What?"

"The British are coming! The British are coming. . . ."

And then he shoves two fingers into my back as he finishes his thought.

"For *you*."

Poke.

You see, Nick the Mimic has been gifted

with the amazing ability to take any class topic . . . I'm talking about *any* class topic since schools were first created in ancient Greek times or whatever . . . and somehow threaten me with it.

Math?

"Bart, bro. Guess what? We all got together and decided to *subtract* you from the school population."

Evolution?

"Hey, Bart! Guess what? You're about to go extinct, along with the rest of the world's boring people!"

And then he'll twist his neck, pop out his tongue, and somehow make this incredibly realistic (and sickening) bone-snapping sound.

Chemistry?

Nick will just stare at me, mouth a silent *boom*, and create a little mushroom cloud with his hands. "That's you, dude. Totally nuked."

Charming guy, my pal Nick. I like to think I'm helping his academic career. If Nick didn't devote his life to making fun of me, I doubt he'd ever pay attention in class.

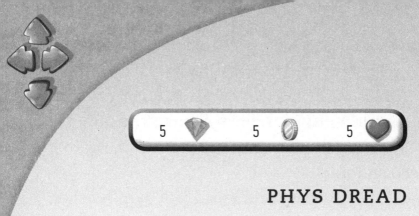

PHYS DREAD

And then there's gym period.

Gym is pretty much the only class where the teacher pays close attention to me. In fact, sometimes it feels like I'm the only kid standing there in the bright, hot sun, waiting to suffer.

This is because my dad is a gym teacher, too. Down the hill at Rancho Verdugo High School he's known as Coach Bill Bean. That's what brought us to this sunbaked wasteland of interesting people in the first place.

Dad is also a serious football junkie. No, seriously—you don't understand. Do you know how most doctors pinch newborn babies to test their reflexes? I'm pretty sure the doc who delivered my dad tossed him a football.

And my dad probably *caught it.*

Bill Bean is such a football nut that he named his only child (*moi*) after his favorite athlete: Bartholomew "Krusher" Kersh, a quarterback with the St. Louis Whatevers.

I grew up with a framed poster of "Krusher" on my wall. I'll be honest: it scared me when I was a little kid. I wondered if my dad put it up to frighten me into doing my homework.

BARTHOLOMEW
"KRUSHER" KERSH

4

Now, Dad knows I'm not into sports. And to his credit, he doesn't push it. But he also thinks I play video games way too much. Back in Philly I'd be sitting there, wrapped up in a killer RPG campaign, and Dad would appear out of nowhere.

"Hey, buddy! How about you close that laptop and head outside with me to throw the old ball around?"

29

(Never mind that there is no "old ball." As a coach, my dad has access to every kind of football, basketball, tennis ball, baseball, soccer ball, bocce ball, pimple ball, and badminton birdie ever created. So I never know what he has in mind.)

"Dad," I'd say, quite reasonably, "I can't shut this off right now or it'll ruin my whole campaign." (A minor fib.)

"Come on, Bart—I know you're able to save those games." (Oops. Busted!)

So, when we moved here to *Rancho El Sunno*, Dad made it a point to become buds with my new gym teacher, who promised my dad he'd help me be more active.

In fact, Coach Pluck has made it his personal mission to turn me into a star athlete just like my dad.

Each time there's class, Coach Pluck presents us with a new "challenge," such as "half push-ups" and "upside-down jumping jacks."

I swear, Coach Pluck must sit up all night thinking about ways to humiliate and demoralize twelve-year-olds with weird "exercises."

And then there's the dreaded "Macaroni Run," in which we have to run around the track as many times as possible in twenty-two minutes or until we collapse to the ground, whichever comes first.

What does macaroni have to do with

running? No idea, but everybody hates it because it pretty much ruins you for the rest of the day.

And sadly, the day is not even halfway done.

6 ♦   6 ◯   6 ♥

THIS BYTES

By lunch period, you'd think I'd be starving—you know, after doing three hundred sideways sit-ups. (Please don't ask me to demonstrate, especially if you're eating.)

But I usually skip the long, depressing cafeteria lines, score a bag of chips, and spend some time on my beloved smartphone.

My phone is my most prized possession. My dad gave it to me for my twelfth birthday this past

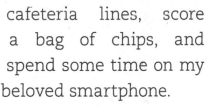

February. I gave him a solemn promise that I wouldn't do anything crazy with it. Like sell vital American secrets to foreign powers or something.

So what *do* I do on my phone during lunch period (and in the mornings, and after school, and before I go bed, and pretty much every chance I get)?

Well, that's a *huge* part of this story, and I'd tell you everything now—I'm not the kind to leave you in suspense—except the *third bully* in my life is approaching. And if I don't take defensive measures now, all will be lost.

WHAT KIND OF CHIPS YOU GOT?

Say hello to Tigran, a.k.a. the Tyrant, my lunch period nemesis. See, YOU have to say hello to the Tyrant, because there is zero chance he's going to say hello to you first. He doesn't do "greetings."

"Plain," I mutter.

"I like sour cream and onion."

I want to say, *There are plenty of bags of sour cream and onion chips for sale over by the snack booth!* But I don't.

The Tyrant helps himself to any of my possessions whenever he feels like it. Pens. Candy bars. A calculator. Whatever.

Or my plain potato chips, even though he's made it clear that he prefers sour cream and onion.

(I *hate* sour cream and onion chips. They remind me of kissing a grandparent who just slurped down a bowlful of sour cream and thought, *Oh, I know—I'll have some raw onions for dessert!*)

Anyway, the Tyrant basically considers me

an ATM machine with a pulse. You don't get to know ATM machines. You don't become friends with ATM machines. You don't say "please" or "thank you" to ATM machines.

You walk up, you take what you want, you leave.

Now, the Tyrant has never threatened me with physical harm or anything (unlike the Golem). He's never made fun of me (unlike the Mimic). No, his preferred terror tactics are much more subtle.

IjustknowthatifIrefusetolettheTyranttake my stuff, something . . . dark . . . unknowable . . . sinister . . . *really awful* will happen.

And yep, that's enough to convince me!

Fortunately, I'm quick enough to hide my beloved smartphone whenever the Tyrant approaches. But I'm more than a little worried that one of these days, I won't see him coming.

THE GIRL WHO . . .

After countless centuries, a half dozen decades, 19 years, 3 months, 2 days, 1.7 hours, 57 minutes, and 4 seconds . . .

The school day is *finally* over.

Fortunately, I live close enough to walk home. Otherwise, I'd have to walk to Rancho Verdugo High School and wait for my dad to finish hanging up jockstraps or inflating footballs or whatever the heck else he does all day. (I kid the old man, he knows that.) While middle school is no picnic, I don't even want to think about the horrors that await me in ninth grade.

Unfortunately, it's still a long, slow slog through the burning sun that pummels the city of *Rancho El Scorcho* relentlessly.

Dad and I live in a pretty cool apartment building, and I'm lucky enough to have my own room. The window looks out onto a little courtyard, which pretty much *everybody* uses.

I mean, everybody passes by my window. Loud kids. Moody teenagers. Cool dudes coming home from a party. Delivery guys. Guys with leaf blowers (even though there are no leaves here in *Rancho Deserto*). It's sort of like living inside the 30th Street Station subway stop back in Philly.

We used to live in a real house back then. Not only did I have my own room, but it was on the second floor *and* faced a tree. The tree never woke me up at 3:00 a.m. telling a dumb joke to its tree buddy.

"So, man, I just told her to leaf! Get it? Get it?"

But I do have one friend in this new apartment complex. Sort of. Kind of.

Maybe?

Whenever I walk through the courtyard, I see a girl, about my age, sitting on the third-floor balcony, right across from my own.

Every day we kind of just . . . look at each other. Me on the ground, her one story up.

She always seems to beat me home from school. Maybe she doesn't have an eighth-period class? Or is she already in high school?

One afternoon, I did something that surprised me. When we looked at each other, I took a chance and . . . waved at her.

And she . . . sort of waved back?

But a second later, she disappeared. Like, instantly. Yikes, did I scare her off her own balcony? Was there something on my face?

I knew nothing about the girl on the balcony, other than she a.) appeared to be a carbon-based life form who breathed air, and b.) had the ability to wave.

And the sad truth was, she was the closest thing I had to a friend.

8 ◆ 8 ◯ 8 ♥

TOP SECRET! PROPER CLEARANCE REQUIRED!

Safe in my bedroom, I opened my laptop. A pale blue glow illuminated the walls. I heard the gentle little whirl of microchips as they began . . . um, *microchipping*.

At long last, I could get on with my *real* work, which I began not long after moving to Rancho Verdugo.

I can't tell you its real name. Not yet. So, for now, just call it . . . oh, I don't know. Something humble like the Most Important Secret Project in the History of the Universe.

Okay, that is kind of a mouthful. So from now on, let's just refer to it as SEC-PRO, for SEC(ret) PRO(ject).

I'm always thinking about SEC-PRO. And I work on it using my beloved smartphone as much as I can during the school day. But to *really* make the magic happen, nothing beats my laptop.

What is this magic you speak of? you may be asking. Well, I can't tell you. Not quite yet. But soon, all will become clear.

The laptop is a hand-me-down from my mom, who gave it to me not long before she split up with Dad. She told me she'd come back for me as soon as she could (I'm not holding my breath) but in the meantime we could stay in touch all the time by Skype or something. This almost never happens, but at least the laptop works.

Anyway, enough of that. I needed to work fast, because Dad would be home soon, and he always grumbles about me being on my laptop. So my plan was to work right up until the moment Pickleback gave me the signal.

Who is Pickleback? you ask.

Pickleback is our dog, and I swear he has superpowers. I'm totally serious. His super-ears can pick up the sound of Dad's car even through several slabs of concrete. The moment Dad's beat-up minivan pulls into the garage, Pickleback goes absolutely *bonkers* with excitement.

EASY,
PICKLEBACK,
THAT TICKLES!

He stampedes through the apartment
(which takes about two seconds) and waits
by the door, tail wagging, booty shaking,
ready to pounce on Dad the moment the door
opens.

Yeah, Pickleback is a little nuts—but he's
an awesome alarm system. Once he goes
tearing off, I have plenty of time to save my

work, close my laptop, then start juggling tennis balls or whatever.

What's that? Oh, the name. Yeah, *Pickleback* was sort of a compromise. Dad wanted to name him after some dumb quarterback or something. I wanted to name him Pickles after nature's perfect food. (Pickles rule; don't try to tell me otherwise. I'll bet they hand out free pickles in Hawaii.) So we came up with something sort of in-between. Pickleback doesn't seem to mind.

But then it was time for work. Pickleback, seeing that I was typing on the dumb plastic thing with all the keys, curled up on my floor and sighed. I opened my SEC-PRO files and started to type. . . .

Then something weird happened. A little box popped up on my screen. It was a friend request from someone.

CyberGirl03 wants to SlapTalk with you! ACCEPT/DECLINE

CyberGirl03? Who the heck was that? Then I remembered: SlapTalk is a messaging app that only works when you're in close range with another SlapTalker. (I tried it out over the summer, only to realize my closest friend was 2,700 miles away.) That meant CyberGirl03 was nearby. *Hmmm.*

I clicked on Accept.

CyberGirl03: Hi.

BoringBart: Um . . .hi?

Hours seemed to pass. Days. Months. Flowers pushed their way up out of the ground and then withered away. . . .

CyberGirl03: You just moved in a few months ago, right?

BoringBart: Yep. Are you the girl on the balcony?

CyberGirl03: Maybe. Where do you come from?

BoringBart: Philadelphia.

CyberGirl03: No. I mean where do you come

from every day, when you walk by?

BoringBart: Oh! School. So you ARE the girl on the balcony?

CyberGirl03: Possibly. And yeah, I figured you were coming home from school. But do you go to Rancho Verdugo Middle or the private one up the road?

BoringBart: Oh. Rancho Verdugo.

BoringBart: Though I'd rather Ver-DON'T-go.

I sucked in my breath. She'd either get my lame pun, or she wouldn't. But a few seconds later she responded:

CyberGirl03: LOL. Good one, Boring Guy.

CyberGirl03: BTW, why is "BoringBart" your handle? You don't seem boring to me.

BoringBart: Trust me, you'll be falling asleep in no time.

CyberGirl03: LOL. I doubt that. I spend most of my time inside my apartment, so believe me, I know all about boring.

BoringBart: Why don't you go to school?

CyberGirl03: I never said I didn't go to school. I do cyberschool. You know, on my laptop?

BoringBart: Which explains YOUR handle.

CyberGirl03: Ding ding ding! We have a winner!

BoringBart: Well . . . I'd better get to work.

CyberGirl03: Homework, huh?

BoringBart: Sort of.

CyberGirl03: What do you mean, sort of? What other kind of work do you do?

Whoops! Already, I'd said too much. I couldn't reveal SEC-PRO to a near-stranger. The beta version is barely even ready!

BoringBart: I mean, I sort of have a lot of homework.

CyberGirl03: So mysterious! Okay, Boring Bart. CU later.

DON'T YOU HAVE A BARN TO RAISE?

Cue: Pickleback, going bonkers. *Woof woof woof woof.*

Cue: Dad, entering the apartment.

Cue: Me, closing my laptop and shoving it under the covers on my bed.

"Bart, buddy—you home?"

I wanted to say, *Um, where else would I be?* But instead I emerged from my inner sanctum, trying to pretend like I haven't been on my laptop for the past ninety minutes.

"It's amazing outside," Dad said. "You want

to hit the pool for a while? Or maybe toss the ol' ball around?"

All I could think was, *In this heat? Are you crazy? Do you want me to spontaneously combust?* But the truth is that I had something else I wanted to show my dad.

"Actually, I was thinking," I said, trying to be as smooth as frozen yogurt, "maybe after dinner I could show you this cool game I found online. All you need is your phone, and you just walk around the apartment looking for . . ."

I stopped talking because of the expression on Dad's face. He looked like I had just suggested that we spend the evening wearing hats made of lettuce while chanting in Klingon.

"A *video game?* Buddy, we just moved to one of the most beautiful places in the country. We should be outside in the fresh air as much as we can."

Here's the thing with Dad. I know he means well. And yeah, maybe he has a good point about going outside more often.

But I wish he'd meet me halfway.

I mean, as far as I know, the old man's never, *ever* picked up a video game controller. Never steered a Mario Kart. Never even cleared a board of Pac-Man. I'm not going to accuse my dad of being a technophobe, but sometimes I think he'd be more comfortable if we all looked like this:

COME ON, BUDDY. THIS BARN WON'T RAISE ITSELF!

The weird thing is, I think my dad would be all about video games if he gave them a chance. I mean, he's a sports fanatic, which means he's into competition, right? I think he'd go crazy with a good MMORPG (massively multiplayer online role-playing game, in case you're a wannabe farmer like my dad).

But the idea of video games boggles poor Dad's mind. "You're always on your electronic devices," he'll say. "Why don't you do something physical? When I was your age . . ."

At which point I'll cut him off, because I've heard the "When I was your age" speech enough times to repeat it backward. And in elvish!

I'll often try to show him whatever game I'm playing, but Dad acts like he's a vampire and I've just shown him a crucifix made of garlic cloves.

Meanwhile, I'm usually too polite to mention how much time my dad spends in front of the flat-screen watching men in puffy uniforms chase each other up and down a field with numbers on it.

I get it. People my dad's age didn't have cool things like cell phones and laptops when *they* were growing up. So they had to make the best of whatever they had lying around.

A LONG, LONG (SERIOUSLY LONG) TIME AGO...

BILL BEAN, WHAT YOU DOING WITH ALL OF THIS JUNK?

BUILDING A GOALPOST. WHAT ELSE ARE WE GOING TO DO UNTIL SOMEBODY GETS AROUND TO INVENTING VIDEO GAMES?

Okay, so maybe it wasn't totally like *that,* but I'm sure it's close.

Anyway, my mission now is to avoid being burned alive. So I told my dad, "I have a lot of homework to catch up on, actually."

"How about just a walk around the neighborhood, then? We've been here three months, and it feels like we haven't had the chance to explore the neighborhood very much."

Again, I wanted to shout: *Go outside? In this roasting, soul-sucking* heat? *Are you kidding?*

Instead I said, "The math alone is probably going to take me an hour or two."

My dad looked disappointed, like I'd just told him he was grounded for a week. I had to throw him a bone.

"Maybe I can walk Pickleback with you later?" I asked. "You know, after dinner." (*And after the skin-blasting, soul-withering sun goes down,* I almost added.)

"Sounds good, buddy. Go on, get to that math. Then we're going outside."

Outside, right.

No.

Wait a minute.

My dad had inadvertently sparked a mini-brainstorm for me. My brain started to spin so fast I could hear it humming inside my skull. *Outside?* Now that was a really interesting idea. . . .

The question was—could I pull it off?

THE END OF ANOTHER RIDICULOUSLY BORING DAY

That night was pretty much like every other night. I finished up my homework. We ate dinner. I put away the dinner dishes. Dad fed Pickleback, and we walked him. Then I told Dad I was pretty tired, and that I wanted to hit the hay to read for a while before falling asleep.

Now even though this has been our nightly routine ever since we moved to *Rancho El Snooze-O*, Dad always seems shocked I don't want to stay up later.

"You sure, buddy? We could watch a few shows or something."

"No, I just want to turn in early," I told him, feeling guilty for fibbing. "Crazy-busy day tomorrow."

"Well, okay."

When I turned to head back to my room, Dad's old football instincts kicked in and he practically *tackled* me. I couldn't help it. I started to giggle and squirm away.

"Ugh, what's with all the PDA, Dad?"

"PD what?"

"PDA. Public Display of Affection."

"Well, for one thing," Dad said, "this is *not* public, so you don't have to worry about me embarrassing you in front of your friends."

As if I have any friends, I want to say, then remembered the Girl on the Balcony, aka CyberGirl03, who clearly didn't have any. Suddenly I felt guilty about even *thinking* that wisecrack. (Boy, the guilt can pile up fast, can't it?)

"And for another thing," Dad continued, "my own dad never liked to hug us before we went off to bed. I always thought that was wrong. So now you're stuck with me hugging you good night for the rest of your life."

I smiled. "Even when I'm extremely old? Like, when I'm in my forties?"

Dad is in his forties. I said this to mess with him.

"Yes," Dad said. "Even when I'm at the impossibly ancient age of fifty. Buddy, even when I'm ninety, I'm still going to want to hug you."

I had no snappy comeback for that one. It was kind of nice to hear that Big, Bad Coach Bill Bean didn't think I was too boring for a hug.

Then I was off to bed (sort of). Thanks to Dad's accidental suggestion, I was going to be up pretty late, working on my laptop.

So there you have it. A typical day in the life of Bartholomew Bean, the Most Boring Middle Schooler in the Universe, right?

Boy, you couldn't be *more* wrong.

11 ◈   11 ◎   11 ♥

BARTHOLOMEW BEAN: MOST IMPORTANT HUMAN BEING IN THE SOLAR SYSTEM

Y̶ou've missed a ton. In fact, you've missed pretty much *everything*.

Let's rewind my typical day and start from the beginning, shall we?

When I wake up in the morning, I don't brush my teeth and think, *Gee, how boring can I possibly be today? Enough to make my classmates pound on me?*

Instead, I'm wondering if I'm going to live

long enough to complete my mission.

See, this is the part you missed. You were focused on the annoying bullies and the weird exercises and my debates with Dad. But the whole time, I had my mind on other things. The most important things you can imagine, in fact.

Can you keep a secret? Here, put your pinky next to mine and swear.

Okay, you're all sworn in. Here's the deal:

I'm a member of a secret society dedicated to keeping order throughout the universe. No, seriously. Our solar system is my beat.

Doesn't sound like much, but do you realize how utterly ginormous the solar system is? If you were to drive to the sun, which is practically around the corner, it would take you 177 years. And the way my dad drives, it would probably take closer to 300 years. (It's the pedal on the right, old man.)

But anyway, I'm based on Earth because that's where all the action happens. Being "boring" is only my cover. And I have to keep my real identity hidden, because I'm the only one who can see the crazy threats that appear *all the time.*

If this secret were to get out, nothing would stand between Earth and utter chaos.

You don't believe me. I can tell. There's a look on your face like you've bitten into a flavored candy and you're not sure if it's coconut or horseradish yet. (Hey, both are chewy.)

That's okay. So let's take a little stroll. I'm supposed to be heading off to school, anyway. Keep up with me, if you can.

Good old Rancho Verdugo looks as sunbaked as ever, right? Palm trees gently swaying. Adults heading off to work. People in uniforms delivering packages. Everybody the star of their own personal reality show.

But take a look at the same scene through the screen on my phone. Can you see it now?

No?

It's right there . . . on top of that traffic light!

That monstrosity right there is a Lerkian, and it's part of an alien race that wants to conquer the universe.

12 ♦   12 ◯   12 ♥

THE SECRET INVASION

Rancho Verdugo is positively *infested* with these little guys. I haven't done a proper census, but according to my calculations, there are about a dozen Lerkians for every human being.

(That's *if* you count people like Giselle the Golem as a human being, but I digress.)

There are so many of them because Lerkians don't invade the usual way—you know, with faster-than-light spaceships and death rays. Instead, they sneak around and mess with all forms of human technology. And I mean *everything*. They attack traffic lights, electric signs, power lines . . . anything with electricity running through it.

But they mess with cell phones, too. Think back to the last time your call was dropped, right in the middle of an important conversation. Or your text mysteriously showed up on some random dude's phone.

You can thank a Lerkian for that.

Don't even get me started on how they screw around with Wi-Fi signals. Lerkians have an uncanny knack for knocking out the internet just when the movie you're streaming hits a really awesome part.

Plus, they have this weird power to be totally invisible to human beings . . . unless you use a certain app that allows you to see them through your smartphone. As of right now, I'm the *only* human being in the world with that app.

So, to recap: the Lerkians show no mercy and want to destroy the world. I'm pretty much the only one who can see them—and potentially stop them. Which is why they so badly want to uncover my secret identity.

To do that, they've enlisted human slaves.

Yep, even poor Giselle the Golem. I don't think she means to be . . . um, *mean*. She must be remote-controlled by the Lerkians,

which is why she's always mindlessly knocking me down. It's an attempt to make me snap and break cover.

Fortunately, I'm able to stay hidden by using my superpower of being unbelievably boring.

13 ♦   13 🪙   13 ♥

MASTER OF STEALTH MODE

I told you that being boring was my cover, right? Fortunately, some allies—and a little bit of futuristic tech—help me maintain that cover.

Remember Mr. Lopez, the homeroom teacher who sometimes forgets to call out my name in class? Die-hard fans of Mr. Lopez (just wait for the action figure; it'll be rad) will be relieved to know that he's probably not forgetting me for real. I believe he's *fake-forgetting*.

Mr. Lopez must know that Lerkians sometimes hide out inside the classroom. They're especially fond of squeezing themselves behind the Smart Board in front of the room. (Which may explain why Mr. Lopez has so much trouble getting the Smart Board to work.)

But anyway, Mr. Lopez isn't skipping my name because he doesn't care. He's probably just helping me stay hidden, making sure that nobody pays much attention to me. Which is the kindest thing anyone could do for me.

Real heroes stay in stealth mode. Deep, deep stealth mode.

Oh, and that thing about nobody noticing me when I raise my hand in class? It's no optical illusion. It's actually a special feature of the Lerkian-hunting app on my phone.

It activates whenever it detects Lerkians in the area. From time to time I'll raise my hand to test it out. If the teacher doesn't call on me, then I know that it's working! I'm invisible, too!

Speaking of allies, remember Nick the Mimic?

I suspect he's not really picking on me. Instead, Nick is most likely giving me top-secret intel in those hints that (supposedly) threaten my life. I listen to every alleged threat and process the *real* message.

For instance, when he says: "Hey, Bart! Guess what? You're about to go extinct, along with the rest of the world's boring people!"

What he really means is: "Hey, Bart, buddy . . . the Lerkians have picked up your scent. Extinct, *stinked* . . . get it? Anyway, watch your six."

Granted, the message doesn't always make sense. But Nick's probably been an

undercover operative here in Rancho Verdugo for a long, long time. And there's always
a good chance the Lerkians have already
scrambled his brains. . . .

BENT OUT OF SHAPE

The sky is suddenly green. And crinkly. Sharp blades press into my palms. I'm dizzy. My feet seem to be floating in the air. It's like the whole world has turned upside down.

Then I remember: *Oh, yeah, I'm in gym, doing an upside-down jumping jack.*

"Keep 'em straight!" Coach Pluck yells. "I want to see those legs doing *perfect elevens!* Elbows *locked!* Face *forward!* Now start banging those feet *together!*"

Elbows? Feet? When you're doing a handstand, your sense of self goes all out of whack. I don't even know if I have real limbs anymore.

But as the blood rushes to my head, I realize that maybe Coach Pluck knows about the alien threat, too. And even his crazy exercises make sense when considering humanity's war with the Lerkians. They don't seem to have real limbs, either.

"Come on, you little buzzards. Push yourself out of your safe little comfort zones! Lemme see some real effort!"

Comfort zones? For once, Coach "Stubborn as a Mack Truck" Pluck is making sense. I think that my gym teacher and all his sideways, backward, and just plain goofy exercises are meant to train my classmates and me for our eventual hand-to-hand combat with the Lerkians.

Or hand-to-creepy-wire-tentacle combat. Whatever, you get the idea.

Despite Coach Pluck's best intentions,

we're not going to win the war against the Lerkians in a massive video game–style brawl. (Though that would be seriously cool.)

I mean, look at them. Duking it out with them would be like getting into a fistfight with a bowl of spaghetti. You have to train your body in an entirely different way if you're hoping to land a punch.

No, humanity has to outsmart the wiry little guys. Which means I have to use that top-secret Lerkian-busting app every chance I get.

Sorry I can't tell you more details about this secret app, or how I found it. The thing is, you—yes, *you,* holding this book in your hands—might be a Lerkian spy.

Don't try to deny it; human double agents are everywhere. Why they—or *you!*—would want the Lerkians to win is beyond me. Some people just like to watch things spin out of control, I guess.

Is that right? Do you enjoy watching civilization crumble?

(Okay, okay . . . I'll ease off. But I'm keeping my eye on you.)

There's no doubt that Tigran the Tyrant is one of those double agents. You've seen the way he swipes my food and supplies. Clearly, this is a tactic meant to slow me down. It's annoying, but I keep a careful eye on him, too.

On *all of you.*

15 ◆ 15 ◯ 15 ♥

THE ALIEN FIGHTER NEXT DOOR

I didn't know it at the time, but one random day in late October would prove to be super-important in my war against the Lerkians.

It ended like most school days: a long walk through the blasting, soul-withering heat (or, as my dad would say: "all of this nice weather"). I made my way to the apartment complex and waved to my only friend—CyberGirl03. She waved back, then held up her smartphone.

Which was her way of saying, "SlapTalk me, okay?"

By the way, there's an important SlapTalk feature I haven't mentioned yet:

Anyway, for those of you who don't keep up with your social media (like my dad, whose idea of "social media" is two soup cans tied together with string), SlapTalk erases your messages sixty seconds after they've been read. Which is super-useful if you happen to be, say, an undercover alien fighter who doesn't want his transmissions falling into the wrong hands. Or claws. Or wire fingers. Or whatever the heck the Lerkians have at the ends of their arms.

The dude who came up with this app is either brilliant or a former spy or both.

He (or she) is, like, my hero. If I could invent something as awesome as SlapTalk, it would make life in Rancho El Verdoo-doo much more tolerable.

Anyway, I opened the SlapTalk app. There was already a message from CyberGirl03 waiting for me.

CyberGirl03: What took you so long? Boy, you move slow.

BoringBart: LOL. What did I miss at the apartment today?

CyberGirl03: Oh, it was terribly thrilling. I counted 17 delivery trucks. And the guy with the leaf blower spent a LOT of time in our courtyard.

BoringBart: LOL.

Yeah, I "laughed out loud." But part of me felt bad for CyberGirl03. Since she does cyberschool at home in her apartment, she doesn't seem to get out very much. She must be bored a lot. I mean, my school days are awful, too—but at least I have bullies to keep things lively.

CyberGirl03: How was your day?

BoringBart: Oh, the usual. Giselle the Golem knocked me over a half dozen times. Nick the Mimic came up with new and interesting threats against my life. On the plus side, I only lost half of my lunch to Tigran the Tyrant.

CyberGirl03: Huh. I didn't know you could have "the Golem" as a last name.

BoringBart: Well, those are sort of my personal nicknames for them.

CyberGirl03: You should fight back. Let them know you can't be pushed around.

BoringBart: But that's the thing. I can literally be pushed around. Especially by Giselle.

CyberGirl03: Well, if I were there, I'd have your back.

The thought of that made me happy and sad at the same time. Happy because it was nice to know I'd have a defender—it'd be nice to have another member of Team Bart. (Pickleback doesn't quite count.)

But sad because CyberGirl03 clearly wanted to be in school. (No idea why she'd want such a thing, but I digress.) I didn't know if she did cyberschool by choice, or if her parents insisted. And I felt weird about bringing it up. So I didn't.

BoringBart: Pretty sure you could take Giselle in hand-to-hand combat.

CyberGirl03: I don't know about that. So what are your big plans tonight, Boring Guy?

I wondered: Could I trust CyberGirl03 enough to tip her off to the Lerkian threat? Would she make fun of me, or recommend that I have a good long chat with someone in a white lab coat?

It would be nice to have another ally in this desperate struggle against the alien hordes. . . .

BoringBart: I actually have a pretty exciting night planned.

CyberGirl03: Let me guess. You have papers

to write for both history AND literature!

BoringBart: HAH. But no. I'm talking about something actually cool.

CyberGirl03: Well then consider me actually intrigued.

BoringBart: Promise you won't share this with anybody else.

CyberGirl03: How can I promise before I know what it is? Maybe it's a cure for some horrible disease. How could I not share something like that?

BoringBart: No, seriously.

CyberGirl03: Okay, okay. I seriously promise.

Not that I didn't trust CyberGirl03, but this was kind of a big deal, letting her into my secret (weird) world.

But now that I'd brought it up, I couldn't back out. I copied the URL to the site where she could download the Lerkian-hunting app, then SlapTalked it to her.

She had sixty seconds to click on it and download the app; otherwise it would disappear forever.

So I hit Send, then waited.

And waited.

And even though it was only thirty seconds, it felt like thirty months had gone by before I saw this reply. . . .

CyberGirl03: Oh, wow! This is an augmented reality game? This is SO COOL! Thank you for sharing with me, Boring Guy!

BoringBart: Sure. :)

CyberGirl03: Where did you find this?

Well, that was the interesting part. . . .

THE BILL BEAN FACTOR

Most of my vital Lerkian-fighting work is done in the evening. Which, of course, is exactly when my dad thinks I should be putting down my "electronic devices" and doing something else with my time.

Parents just love that phrase, don't they? Is it too difficult to say "phone" or "laptop"?

And as far as doing something else with my time—something "productive" (which is another one of his favorite words)—what exactly might that be? Throwing an inflated chunk of pigskin back and forth? I've never understood that. Nothing new ever comes out of that. It's just throwing an inflated chunk of pigskin back and forth, back and forth, back and forth. . . .

So I was forced to go underground to continue my work. Or make that under *covers,* since that's the best place to hide my laptop. The only problem is Pickleback, who thinks I'm playing a game and tries to crawl under there with me.

But Pickleback isn't the only problem; it's Dad. He tries to catch me on my laptop at odd times. He thinks he's clever. Fortunately, Dad's version of clever dates to the 1800s. He's not anticipating modern technology.

A few weeks ago I bought a device online (with my allowance money, mind you . . . nothing shady going on here). This device looks like a tiny plastic square. It's tan, and coincidentally, the same shade of tan as the walls in our apartment. (Note: this is not a coincidence.) One side is flat and plain. The other has a little peel-off sticker that allows you to put it anywhere. Like, say, six inches from the floor, where Dad won't see it.

Especially when he walks down the hallway to come check on me.

The instant he walks by that tiny plastic square, an alert is sent to my laptop. A message appears on my screen:

DAD APPROACHING.
DAD APPROACHING.
DAD APPROACHING.

(It's not a red alert until it is displayed three times.)

Immediately, I save my work and spring into action.

By the time Dad is in my doorway, I'm looking like I've been diligently catching up on some fascinating math problems. A second later, I notice that the textbook in my hands is, um, upside down.

"Hey, Bart. Why don't you give homework a rest and come walk with me. I want to take the dog out for a while."

"Seriously?" I reply. "It's eleven billion degrees outside!"

"No, the sun's going down. It's a lot cooler. C'mon, it'll be fun."

Now "fun" is not the word I'd use to describe a walk up and down Verdugo Boulevard with Pickleback stopping every 3.7 seconds to see if any of the other dogs in the neighborhood have left him any messages. If Pickleback were human and had email, he'd be one of those people who hit Refresh on his browser every two seconds.

"Sorry, Dad, I really should get back to

these math problems." I hope Dad hasn't noticed that I've used a little sleight of hand to flip the textbook right side up.

"What if I say we can stop for some Frosty's Freeze at the end of the walk?"

Ooooh—Dad's breaking out the big guns now. He knows the one thing I can't resist is a cone full of dairy-based frozen bliss. But resist, I must. My work on our ultimate defense against the invading Lerkians must continue, no matter what.

So I force myself to spit out the words: "I'm really . . . not that hungry."

"Okay, buddy. Just thought I'd ask." The disappointment in his voice hurts me just as much as missing out on that ice cream.

But I can't stop my work—especially now that CyberGirl03 has joined the hunt for the Lerkian invaders!

THE MOST IMPORTANT WORK IN THE SOLAR SYSTEM, AND POSSIBLY BEYOND

So, what, exactly, is all of this important work? What could possibly compel me to pass up a cone of Frosty's Freeze, complete with hot fudge and sprinkles? (Still regretting that, by the way . . .)

Well, it's simple. I've been coding.

You know—*computer coding.*

And right now, I'm hearing a record needle slide off the edge of the LP. The set of drums tumbling down the stairs, and a final, pathetic cymbal crash. A million voices crying out, *"That's it? That's the important work you've been doing?"*

Well . . . yeah.

Look, I know it sounds boring. But trust me—this work is *essential*. Coding is what makes of all those "electronic devices" do stuff. In fact, everything you enjoy in this world is thanks to nerds like me who slam together numbers and letters and symbols.

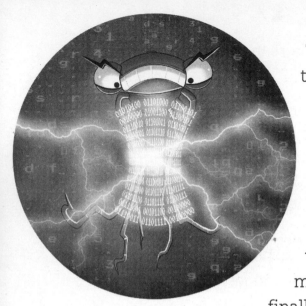

The Lerkians target our technology, so the only way to fight back is with even better technology. And after all these long (hot) months, there's finally an app that will take them all down!

Namely . . . um, the app on my smartphone. You know, the one I shared with CyberGirl03 earlier? The game I hoped my dad would check out (and good luck with that one)?

Well, I'm constantly coding because . . . *I created the app.*

WAIT WHAT

Now, *shhhhhh!* Don't tell anyone!

I practically can hear you screaming at this page:

What about the stuff about Lerkians and mind-control and weird exercises and alien invasions? Did you make all that up, too, hoping to hide the fact that you are completely boring in real life?

Yes, the Lerkians are totally fake. They're figments of my imagination. I wanted to create an augmented reality game set in my own apartment starring these creepy little creatures who would cause all kinds of mayhem.

BUSTED.

And then my dad kept harping on me about going outside, so I thought: *Wait. Why not set the game outside, too?* Imagine unleashing the Lerkians on all of Rancho Verdugo? Admit it: the place seriously had it coming.

Actually, Dad was the one who inspired the game in the first place.

18 ◆   18 ◯   18 ♥

CODING'S NOT SO BORING NOW, IS IT?

I've been slowly building this game ever since Dad moved us here in the summer. What else did I have to do? So, every free moment I had, I was coding. On my phone at school? Coding. On my laptop in the evening? Coding. Brushing my teeth in the morning? I'm thinking about coding. Eating breakfast? Ditto.

Even when I'm *actually coding,* I'm thinking about the coding I'm going to be doing tomorrow.

From the day we arrived in hot, dusty Rancho Verdugo I'd been dreaming of creating my own virtual game. The people who make this stuff are my heroes. And  honestly, it wasn't that hard to pick up. Once you start playing around with a few lines of code, it's hard to stop.

And the next thing you know, you're plotting an alien invasion. It just kinda happens.

Yeah, okay—I'll admit it. I was superbummed about having to move to a new city and attend a new school. It's not Dad's fault—nobody's fault, really. But it's tough being pulled away from everything and everyone you know.

So I thought: *What if I create little creatures that cause things to go, well, haywire?*

Soon, I was wondering what kind of alien life form would thrive in this hostile environment, and, one hot August day, the image of a Lerkian popped into my head. All squishy and spindly, like a tumbleweed.

I was inspired when Dad drove me past one of those inflatable blow-up guys—you know, with the waving arms and crazy hair—that they stick in front of shops to attract attention.

What can I say? It was a way to keep my mind off the crummy realities of my new life. With every piece of code, I was taking my revenge on *Rancho Verdidn't Want to Move Here.*

Sadly, all this coding (and thinking about coding) is why everybody thinks I'm so boring. In reality, my brain is bursting with alien action and how to make it look as realistic as possible. You wouldn't believe how much time (and noodle-power) that takes.

So, boring? Please. On any given day, I'm the most exciting person in the room!

But I could have never guessed what would happen next.

THE DAY OF THE HECKLR

If you were to ask someone about the moment when everything changed in Rancho Verdugo, they'd probably tell you it was one day in late October.

A Tuesday, in fact. Lunch period.

Two kids were in my cafeteria a few tables away, ignoring their food and looking at their phones (as kids do). To protect the innocent, let's call these two gentlemen . . . oh, I don't know . . . Clueless Chuck and Eagle-Eyed Eduardo.*

(*Any resemblance to actual persons,

living or dead, is purely coincidental, and not because these two goofballs once tripped me during gym.)

Eduardo said to Chuck, "Have you seen this heckle thing?"

"What?"

"This new game. Hecklr or something. It's a free download. Somebody sent it to me. It says I'm supposed to scan the room or something."

"Quit bugging me. I'm in the middle of an important SlapTalk."

"Whoa! This is the coolest!" Eduardo exclaimed, looking at his screen while pointing his phone at Chuck. "There's one right on top of your head!"

Now this got ol' Clueless Chuck's attention. "Wait, what? Is there something on my hair?" (Dude likes his hair to be *just so*.)

"Hahahahaha! It's taking apart your phone!"

Now people were starting to gawk at Chuck and Eduardo, wondering what the fuss was all about. All they saw was Eduardo holding his phone up to Chuck, and poor Chuck patting his head, wondering if someone had spilled some fettuccine Alfredo on his golden locks.

I was looking at them, too, kind of stunned. I was pretty sure I knew what Eduardo saw on his screen. And it would be something like this:

After a few minutes, other kids were looking over Eduardo's shoulder to see what kind of game he was playing.

Word spread quickly through the cafeteria: It's a sci-fi augmented reality game called Hecklr. Not only does it sound cool, but it's a completely free download. And it works on pretty much any smartphone with a built-in camera manufactured after, say, 1887 (or whenever smartphones were invented).

I was freaking out. More than a little. How did Eduardo find the link to the app? Did someone tip him off?

I mean . . . that was my game!

Though I have to admit, it was kind of fun to watch everybody at lunch period take out their phones and start downloading like crazy. They were pointing their phones at each other, at the walls, at the cafeteria ladies (who are *not* impressed, not by a long shot), and giggling like mad.

So I did the same thing, downloading a

copy of my own game to my own beloved phone. (Hey, I have to make sure it's working right!)

The app asked me for a username (whoops, forgot I added that feature), so I went with the only one that made sense: "UBoringBart02."

The 02 is for my birth month, which is February. The U is for the word "Unbelievably." It felt appropriate, somehow.

And with the selection of a password . . . the adventure began!

20 ◆   20 ◯   20 ♥

THEY'RE HEEEERE . . . AND THERRRRRE . . . AND PRETTY MUCH EVERYWHERE

The cafeteria was already full of players, so I stepped into the hallway. The bell was still a few minutes away from ringing, so for the moment all was quiet.

Except . . .

I held up my smartphone and there they were!

Two Lerkians, clinging to the ceiling and pulling apart the fixtures. Sparks popped and rained down on the linoleum floor. Through my phone's speakers I could hear a creepy little laugh. It was in their alien language, which means it's basically unpronounceable by human beings. But if I had to give it my best guess, it would sound something like:

XEE-XEE-XEE!!! XEE-XEE-XEE!!! XEE-XEE-XEE!!!

When I lowered my phone, the two Lerkians disappeared IRL (that would be "in real life," in case you're an Amish farmer . . . or my dad). You could only see them—and hear their weird little giggle—through the display of the game.

XEE-XEE-XEE!!! XEE-XEE-XEE!!! XEE-XEE-XEE!!!

And everyone else playing the game right then was experiencing the same thing. When they held up their phones and looked at the world through the built-in cameras, they could see the Lerkians attacking pretty much *anything* that uses electricity.

Computers. Watches. Neon signs. Earphones. Security cameras. Video game consoles. Cars. TVs. Entire *skyscrapers*, people.

Anything that uses modern technology is prey to these wiry little creepazoids.

Seeing the Lerkians is great and all. But what the heck are we supposed to *do* about them? Or are we doomed to a world without anything that runs on electricity?

Nope.

Once you've got a Lerkian (or two) in your

sights, you tap a button to *lock on* to them. For a few seconds, they won't be able to move. Not even one single little wire.

And then you type in a verbal warning in a little text box on your screen.

So I typed:

> **Hey! You two get off that ceiling right this very instant!**

The Lerkians just stared back at me through the screen. (Did I mention they're super-creepy when they look you in the eye?) I made the classic newbie mistake: I wasn't insulting them creatively.

As long as you don't use the kind of "creative" language that would get your uncle kicked out of the house during Thanksgiving. You know what I mean. Let's be grown-ups here; we're alien-fighting, after all!

So I tried something else:

Yo, spaghetti faces! I'm your worst nightmare!

The Lerkians turned to gawk at each other, then they did a little scaredy-pants dance, and finally they scurried away as fast as their whip-like legs (arms?) could carry them.

STOP THEM BEFORE THEY STOP US!

After school, during my usual hot slog through the arid wastelands of *Rancho El Heck No,* I came upon an amazing sight:

Five of my classmates were gathered around a big neon sign for JOEY G'S BACK TO THE 50S DINER. They pointed their phones up at the sign as if it were an alien artifact and they were space explorers sent out to analyze it.

Meanwhile, there were some midafternoon customers at tables out front, snacking on french fries and sodas and staring at the middle schoolers gathered under the neon sign.

"Something wrong?" one of the customers asked.

"Can't you see them?" one of the students responded. "There have to be at least a dozen up there."

"A dozen what?"

"A dozen of them."

"Them? Them *who?*"

Meanwhile, I lifted my own phone to the neon sign and . . . wow. They weren't kidding. It was a crazy infestation of Lerkians, who clung to the sign like a bunch of ants who have discovered a splotch of ice cream on the sidewalk.

WOO-HOO ICE CREEEEEEAAAMMMMM!

(At least, that's what I imagine ants would say after stumbling upon a mountain of fudge ripple.)

But these Lerkians, man, they really seemed to love their neon.

"They're not responding to my threats," one of the students said.

"Not to mine, either. Maybe I'm not being funny enough?"

"So, what are we supposed to do?"

A customer looked at my classmates. Then up at the sign. Then back at my classmates.

He blinked. "Are you kids feelin' all right?" Everybody ignored him.

I coughed. Everyone—classmates, customers—turned in my direction. *Oops. I guess I'd better say something.*

"Um, hey," I stammered. My skin suddenly felt cold, even though I was standing beneath the punishing heat of the Rancho Verdugo sun. "I heard that if a bunch of players focus on a single Lerkian at a time, and then shout at the same time, it might scare all of them away."

"Who'd you hear that from?" one of the students demanded.

"Hey, who cares?" said another. "It's worth a try."

"The one in the middle, on top of the G. Focus on that one."

"Okay, cool."

"Got 'im!"

"Me, too."

"Give him everything you've got!"

All my classmates were typing furiously, hurling noiseless PG-rated insults at this little Lerkian, who started to shiver and shake. *Why is everybody picking on me?*

Sure enough, the Lerkians all began to

scatter, heading for less hostile ground. The group effort worked! Shockingly! I mean, ask any student for the two most dreaded words in the middle school language and they pretty much have to be:

GROUP PROJECT

(I just sent a shiver down your spine, didn't I?)

But in this case, the group project was a huge hit. Everyone gave each other high fives. The poor customers of Joey G's Back to the 50s Diner, however, were completely baffled. *Have all the kids in this city lost their minds at the same time?*

That's actually not too far from the truth.

22 ♦   22 ◉   22 ♥

MEANWHILE, BACK AT THE
RANCH(O). . .

Within a week, Hecklr mania had spread like crazy, much to my complete surprise.

Heck (see what I did there?), I created this game to amuse myself. When my dad started complaining that I didn't do enough outdoor activities, I designed the game so you could play it outdoors. In fact, you could play it *anywhere* within Rancho Verdugo city limits that had something powered by electricity.

But fat luck getting Coach Bean to look at a screen.

I uploaded the game to the internet so that CyberGirl03 could give it a try. I thought it would make her laugh, and maybe less bored during the day.

Now it seems like everybody at my middle school is hunting for Lerkians—including some *teachers*. No, I'm being completely serious. Now when Dad drops me off in front of the school every morning, I see at least two teachers (Hello, Mr. Southward, hey there, Miss Rice) pointing their phones at the big electric RANCHO VERDUGO MIDDLE SCHOOL sign.

I wonder what my teachers say to the little alien creepazoids to make them go away. Is it the same kinds of things they say to us students?

I can imagine Coach Pluck trying to whip the Lerkians into shape.

But the mania has spread far beyond the walls of my school. People all over the city are wandering the streets, phones in their hands laughing and pointing. It's like a zombie invasion, minus the zombies!

Sometimes, traffic grinds to a halt as players with their cell phones wander into the street in an attempt to stop the Lerkians from committing another dastardly deed. And the people who have to pull their cars over? Well, they don't really mind, because it gives them an excuse to take a break and stop another Lerkian!

Now, I can imagine how scary this must seem to people who haven't heard about Hecklr. They must think the general population has gone out of its mind. Maybe somebody dumped some kind of mind-control superdrug into the drinking water! Maybe aliens are actually invading!

And I'm guessing that one or two of these concerned citizens called the local TV news stations, because suddenly there are reporters and cameras on the streets, interviewing random Hecklr players.

"Excuse me, miss—Tom Giacchino, Action News. Are you currently playing Hecklr?"

"OMG—there's one on your camera! Don't you see it?"

"Are you being serious, miss? I don't see anything."

"Here, look through my phone!"

"*Gah!* You're right! How do I get rid of it?"

Meanwhile, the camera guy starts freaking out. "Get it off me! Get it off me!"

And then viewers at home are treated to shaky-cam footage of Tom Giacchino as he tries to insult the Lerkian enough so that it will leave his poor camera guy alone.

ACTUALLY, IT'S KIND OF CUTE

Stuff like this is just born to go viral. And guess what: *it does.*

Within a few days, everybody seemed to know about Rancho Verdugo, California, the capital of Hecklr mania. For some mysterious (*ahem*) reason, the Lerkians are really focused on this small town just outside of sunny Los Angeles.

Soon, people were asking why the game didn't work in other parts of the country. Did the company behind Hecklr do a "soft" roll-out to see how the game would do in a tiny little sunbaked place like Rancho Verdugo?

And if that was the case, when would it be available in New York City? Topeka, Kansas? Wilkes-Barre, Pennsylvania? Truth or Consequences, New Mexico?

And more importantly—who was behind this game? No company seemed to be taking credit for it, which drove people bonkers. What the heck was going on?

(Heh heh heh.)

Tourists started pouring into Rancho Verdugo just to play Hecklr. I'm not kidding! They were spending buckets of money just to fly here and chase around little wiry aliens on their smartphones.

And as for me? Well, I never felt happier.

In those early days of Hecklr mania, I would walk around the streets of my adopted city, thrilled to see everyone playing *my* game.

But I never, *ever* reveal my secret.

SHHHHH

Right about now you might be asking yourself:

WHY?

Why *wouldn't* I want to take credit for this game? I mean, for all the good I've done for Rancho Verdugo's tourist industry, they should throw a parade and hand me the key to the city, right?

Heck, they probably make me mayor of this boiling desert town!

But I didn't create Hecklr to get famous. Please! If the truth were to come out, life as I know it would be over. I'd be forced to do interviews, set up all kinds of boring business stuff, hang out with celebrities . . . ugh. Who'd want to put up with that? I'd have to move way and hide somewhere far away . . . like Hawaii.

(Hey, maybe that's not such a bad idea!)

Okay, in all seriousness: I'm a little on the shy side. That's why coding rules. You don't have to talk to anybody! Ever! Except for the few super-important people in your life. I don't need a billion friends. I'd just like have . . . one? Two maybe?

Fame? No thanks, man. All I wanted was for people to have fun with this game.

Okay, maybe a *certain* person.

THE BILL BEAN FACTOR, PT. 2

This whole city has gone crazy."

This was my dad, a.k.a. Bill Bean, speaking. He always thinks the city, the country, the world (or whatever) is going crazy. But it appeared he really meant it this time.

"Bart, you're never going to believe what I saw driving home from school today," Dad continued. "People are acting like zombies! I had to stop the car three times to make sure I didn't run somebody over. And then . . . *and then . . . !*"

(Dad was getting pretty revved up now. He tends to repeat the phrase *"and then!"* for emphasis, even though the first "and then!" worked just fine.)

". . . some people actually gathered around my car and pointed their phones at me! I had no idea what they were doing."

I mumbled, "Maybe they were trying to save you?"

"Huh? Save me from what?"

"Um, aliens," I told him.

"What? Bart, are you okay?" Dad reached over and felt my forehead. "Are you running a temperature?"

"Dad, I'm fine."

"Let me find the thermometer . . ."

"Wait—I'm not sick."

Patiently, I explained to my dad the concept of this online augmented reality game called Hecklr. Only, I didn't call it a "virtual reality game." Instead, I told him Hecklr is a new kind of *outdoors challenge* that requires your smartphone. I even used sports-y words that I thought he'd respond to.

"People can *team up* to fight the Lerkians, Dad! Or *players* can try to combat them *one-on-one*. The *goal* is simple: the more aliens you chase away, the more *points* you get."

But Dad was still hung up on a word I used earlier. "Did you say . . . *aliens?*"

Oof. He didn't hear a word I said.

LIKE FROM OUTER SPACE?

So I tried another strategy:

"I heard it's pretty rad. Want to go outside and try it out for yourself?"

Nothing doing. Bill Bean shook his head. "Since when did you need a cell phone to go outside and run around and have fun? Sounds like a huge waste of time!"

Ugh, and then we were off on another Bill Bean Lecture™ about how "electronic devices" were the downfall of modern civilization or whatever. I used the opportunity to tune out and do a little mental coding.

But then Dad looked at me. "Bart."

"Yeah, Dad?"

"*You're* not playing that stupid game, are you?"

"Um . . ."

NOPE. NOT ME. UH-UH.
NO WAY.

A few days later, I was walking home after school through the scorched wasteland of El Rancho Verdugo when something weird started happening.

Plink.

I blinked, then touched my face. No. It couldn't be. I looked up, wondering if any Lerkians had somehow escaped their cyber-world and made it into the real world. And

now they were seeking revenge on their creator.

But there were no Lerkians to be seen.
And then it happened again. And again. And
again!

Plink. Plink. PLOP.

Right on the top of my head with a fat
messy splat. Alert the media, people—it was
raining in Rancho Verdugo.

You have to understand something about my new city. It's been under a severe drought watch for something like 7,438 years (give or take). My dad explained that was an unfortunate drawback to living in a "beautiful" and "sunny" place with nice weather all of the time.

So when it rains here it catches everybody by surprise. Including me, who hasn't packed an umbrella since I left my hometown back in Pennsylvania (where it rains pretty often, especially when you want to go outside).

I ran for it.

Luckily, I was only a few blocks away when the deluge began. Okay, so maybe it wasn't exactly a flood. But my T-shirt was sort of vaguely damp by the time I reached the apartment complex. I brushed the rain out of my hair as I approached CyberGirl03's balcony.

But she wasn't there. Huh. I thought

maybe the sudden rainstorm forced Cyber-Girl03 back inside her apartment.

As it turned out, she wasn't staying dry. She was catching Lerkian invaders.

CyberGirl03: We're in serious trouble, Boring Guy.

BoringBart: We are?

CyberGirl03: We're under attack!

BoringBart: Nah, that's just rain.

CyberGirl03: Ha, ha. No, you know those Lerkian things? Well our apartment complex is pretty much crawling with them! I've got one trying to eat the camera on my computer.

BoringBart: I don't think they eat anything. They just destroy stuff? I think?

CyberGirl03: What do you mean, you think? You're the one who first showed me this game!

BoringBart: Well, there are hardly any Lerkians in my apartment. Guess they don't like me much.

Heh heh heh.

This is a fib, because I control the number of Lerkians in Rancho Verdugo and where they appear. If I wanted, I could fill my entire bedroom with wall-to-wall Lerkians.

I knew that CyberGirl03 stayed at home a lot, so I made sure there was plenty of alien action for her to tackle right in her own bedroom.

But me? Play the actual game?

I didn't have time. I was too busy trying to keep the game from collapsing under the weight of all these new players!

BART FALL DOWN, GO BOOM

Despite all the Hecklr hoopla, my troubles at school really didn't change all that much. I was still forgettable ol' boring . . . what's that kid's name again? I was the loser who kept to himself, typing on his phone instead of playing sports or goofing around with friends or chasing Lerkians around the school property.

(Little does anyone know I'm *coding like crazy* just to keep the game running smoothly.)

And in some ways, the game only made them worse.

My hallway nemesis, Giselle the Golem, became a huge Hecklr fan. You would think this would be a good thing, right? The Lerkians should be keeping her too busy to smash into me in the hallway.

Well, you would be wrong.

Because now Giselle, staring at her phone, was *more* oblivious.

She knocked me down like a bowling pin responsible for the death of the bowling ball's best friend . . . or something.

So I was forced to improvise. Whenever there was even the *slightest* chance of a Giselle sighting on campus, I would quickly order all the Lerkians to be somewhere else—the gym, the cafeteria, the Griffith Observatory, Uzbekistan, wherever.

Genius, right?

Wrong.

This just meant that Giselle would be in an even *bigger* hurry to get to the gym, the cafeteria, the Griffith Observatory, or wherever. And for Giselle, the shortest distance between two points is not a straight line. It's a line that has *me* in the middle. She's like a heat-seeking missile, twisting and turning through the air as she seeks out her moving target . . .

Me.

She routinely crashed into me like she was a safety test vehicle and I was a crash test dummy.

I guess I could look on the bright side: Giselle was obviously a fan of the game. Which was, in a twisted way, flattering. I wonder what would happen if I told her that I was the guy who created the *whole thing*, down to the last Lerkian?

Who am I kidding? I'd probably get three words out of my mouth—

"Hey, Giselle, guess wh—"

Before—

El smacko.

And I'd be smooshed into the linoleum tile of the school hallway.

27 ◈   27 ◯   27 ♥

ERROR MESSAGE 3740:
YOU STINK

H ey."
     I felt a hard poke in the middle of my back. At that moment I was pretending to pay attention to American history while thinking about all of the super-serious coding I had waiting for me during lunch period. The life of a brilliant secret game designer is not an easy one.

Then came another poke. One that I'm pretty sure bruised my spinal column.

"Hey."

I didn't turn around because I knew who was poking me: Nick the Mimic. Somehow, he knows to pick on me at the worst possible moments.

"Hey, Bartholo . . . *stew*," he says. "I'm *talking* to you."

That was Nick's new gag: ridiculous variations on my first name. It started a week ago when Mr. Lopez, our homeroom teacher, remembered (for once!) to call out my name. For some reason he didn't just say, *Bean?* He said my whole name: *Bartholomew Bean?*

I cringed, because at that same moment I saw Nick's eyes light up as if someone had given him a billion dollars. Because for the next few days, all I heard was:

"Hey, Bartholo . . . *poo*."

"Hey, Bartholo . . . *glue*."

"Hey, Bartholo . . . *pew!*"

(I guess I should have been grateful that

he didn't play around with variations of my shortened first name, Bart. Yes, I know. Please don't go there.)

I couldn't take it anymore. I turned around and yell-whispered: *"What? What do you want?"*

"You're always on your phone," Nick said

oh so casually, as if we were just hanging out, shooting the breeze.

"So are you," I replied, trying not to raise my voice above a harsh whisper. "So is everybody. Who cares?"

"No," Nick said. "All of us normal people are on our phones playing Hecklr. But you're just on your phone doing . . . well, what *are* you doing? Why aren't you catching aliens like the rest of us?"

I turned back around. I couldn't tell him the truth—that I designed the game—so I decided to say nothing at all.

"What, are you too good to play? Got better things to do? Bartholo . . . *pew! pew! pew!*"

With every fake laser-blast sound came another poke, harder than the one before. I wished I could order a team of Lerkians to drop from the ceiling, tangle Nick up in a huge ball, and roll him like a tumbleweed up into the Verdugo Mountains.

Because here's the problem: Hecklr is super-popular. Way more than I ever expected, actually. I really thought that maybe, *maybe* . . . *best case* . . . CyberGirl03 and a couple of other nerds would discover it and play around with it for a while. I had no idea that Lerkian-mania would sweep through the entire school. No idea that *teachers* would become obsessed with tracking down aliens.

But with so many people logged on to the game, I'm always checking my phone to deal with all the system bugs that have been popping up.

And with a game that pretty much covers all of Rancho Verdugo, there are only a gazillion bugs to be fixed.

So why am I not "catching aliens like the rest of us," Nick? Believe me, that would be awesome, if I had a microsecond of free time. I don't even have time to do homework like I used to.

And as much as teachers tend to think I don't exist, it's only a matter of time before *somebody* notices.

28 💎   28 🪙   28 ❤️

THE LERKIANS MAKE FRIENDS

I had another problem: people were starting to play Hecklr in a weird, backward kind of way.

I call it "double agent mode," and it was definitely *not* something I had originally programmed into the game.

See, there are some players (I've discovered) who actually think the Lerkians are "cute." Oh, yeah. I read the comments people leave for the game. And my jaw drops open when I see stuff like:

They're just precious little
tumbleweed monsters! A treasure,
not a menace.

Awwww, they're just widdle
babies who need to be protected!

Let's not scare them away! Let's
save them all!

Yeah! How about we team up
to protect them from all the
meanies in Rancho Verdugo?

I, for one, welcome my new
Lerkian overlords.

This, people, is why you should never, *ever*
read the comments section. People may think
the Lerkians are cute, but I'd love to see you
try to hug one of them. Ick.

But anyway, some players began protecting the little Lerkian jerks. Hence, "double agent mode." They'll pretend to be on the good guys' side for a while, helping to shoo away some of the aliens from, say, an electronics store.

(Lerkians *love* to snack on smartphones, BTW. It's like popcorn to them!)

But secretly, these double agents are actually *encouraging* the Lerkians, helping them avoid the other human players and showing them other devices they can attack. When I programmed the game, I never imagined that someone would actually want to assist the little buggers in their quest for technological domination.

People are weird.

All of which means there are *more* bugs for me to deal with. Double agents soon discovered that helping the Lerkians made them really powerful. And sometimes, the Lerkians "win," completely shutting down a game location—I'm talking total devastation. Until I can get it up and running again, that is.

So in addition to trying to keep up with all of the system bugs, I had to deal with the double agent problem. Which meant that most days I was too busy to talk with CyberGirl03.

CyberGirl03: Are you busy catching aliens, mister boring guy?

BoringBart: No, HAH.

CyberGirl03: You should have seen the one that was trying to rip apart our TV. That took some serious talking to get him to finally go away. I called him a "scroodly-oodly noodle brain." That got his attention.

BoringBart: Wow.

CyberGirl03: So what are you up to?

BoringBart: Nothing much.

CyberGirl03: I get the feeling that I am bothering you.

BoringBart: No, sorry, just busy with a lot of homework.

CyberGirl03: Got it.

Honestly, I wanted to say more than two words to CyberGirl03, but I happened to be in the middle of some particularly gnarly debugging. I tried reaching out to her later, but either she was away from her phone—or she'd taken my contact information, printed it out, carried it into the courtyard, then set it on fire.

Worst of all, I only had myself to blame. There I go, dissing my only real friend in this city!

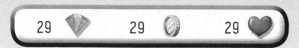

29 ◆   29 ◎   29 ♥

BIG TROUBLE IN EL RANCHO

Dad returned home from work one day just as I was struggling with the latest round of Hecklr bugs. It was getting to the point where I'd blink and see nothing but numbers and symbols on the inside of my eyelids.

Pickleback's loud barks gave me plenty of warning about Dad's imminent arrival, but I was still bummed to have to put away my work. I had SO much to do!

Dad peeled off his baseball cap and threw it onto the dining room table. Something was wrong. He looked like someone had swiped his favorite catcher's mitt, or whatever. (Sorry, I'm not good with sports metaphors.)

"You'll never believe what's going on at the school next week," Dad said.

"What's that?" I asked, half-listening just to be polite. I had my own problems to deal with. What kind of trouble could Coach Bean possibly have? Did someone put chili pepper in the jock straps? Were the soccer balls under-inflated during the big game? Whatever it was, it didn't compare to my daily coding nightmares.

"You know that stupid game? With the aliens and stuff?"

Now *this* had my attention. "Uh, do you mean Hecklr?" (That is to say, the game I totally *never* play and completely *didn't* invent, as far as you know, Dad?)

"Yeah. That one. With the monsters that look like dental floss."

That wasn't exactly fair to the Lerkians, but I ignored the insult for the moment. "What about it?"

"Because of that stupid game, I'm going to have to take all of my gym classes *inside* for a full week."

I felt a tiny knot in my stomach, but I didn't quite know why. "What do you mean, inside? What's wrong with the field?"

"They've commandeered the field all week long to set up the stage, monitors, cameras, and whatnot."

"For what?"

Dad blinked. "You mean you didn't hear? Some cable channel about video games is coming to Rancho Verdugo to broadcast a special about that dumb game. They're going to have kids playing it live."

WHAT!

Inside, my heart started pumping like a kick drum in a techno song. I felt dizzy. I understood what my dad had said, but the words stubbornly refused to make total sense in my brain. Video game channel? The game? Broadcast? *Live?*

Dad must have noticed that my face suddenly took on the appearance of very old cottage cheese. "Bart, buddy, you okay?"

I tried to recover as best I could. "Yeah, I'm

fine, Dad. Just got a lot of homework piling up."

"Well," Dad said, "I was going to take Pickleback up to Frosty's for a little snack. You want to come along with us?"

"I really should get back to work." (Which was the truth. Sort of.)

"Homework can wait. I'm a teacher, too, you know. And sometimes a break can help you do better work."

"Can you bring me back something?"

"And what, juggle two soft-serve cones and a crazy dog? I don't think so. C'mon, walk with me. You don't want to disappoint Pickleback, do you?"

We go out, and Pickleback *does* go crazy for Frosty's soft-serve. We pretend we're "sharing" one of our cones with him, but Dad only has a lick or two before surrendering the rest to the pooch.

You should see the look in Pickleback's eyes. He's all like:

Really? I can have a lick? For real? Oh, wow . . . wait . . . I can have another lick? You are sure? Well, okay, if you'll let me . . .

And in a matter of seconds Pickleback has licked the soft-serve clean down to the cone. Which he then chomps in half. And before Dad can say, "Whoa, Pickleback, take it easy—"

Chomp goes the other half. It's pretty awesome.

But then I started thinking about all the coding I had to do tonight. Suddenly, the soft-serve tasted sour to me. I didn't have time for frozen treats. I didn't have time for anything else.

"You okay, buddy?" my dad asked.

For a second I wanted to tell him the truth. But I could easily imagine Dad freaking out and making me take the whole game down. Which would disappoint the entire city, not to mention CyberGirl03.

"Yeah, Dad. Just have a lot of homework waiting for me."

Dad nodded. "I know how you feel. When work piles up it can feel overwhelming. So, what you do is take a deep breath and make a list. Tackle one thing at a time. The world won't fall apart in the meantime."

I couldn't help it. Dad meant well, but in

this case he had no idea what he was talking about. Make a list? Was he being serious? Making a list of all the bugs I had to fix would pretty much take me all night.

And then I'd still have to deal with the bugs!

"What's due first, bud?" Dad continued. "English? Social studies? Math?"

"Dad!" I yelled. "Stop, please. That's not going to help!"

My dad looked like I'd shoved my ice cream cone in his face. And I felt *awful* about it. (Even Pickleback looked at me, confused.) I know he was just trying to help, but he couldn't.

"Okay," he finally said. "I know you'll get it all done. But I'm here if you need me."

As we walked home I felt like the gross slime at the bottom of a river. I could imagine a gang of Lerkians hanging off power lines and traffic lines, pointing at me and laughing.

What a dope! This world is pretty much ours!

30 ◆　　　30 ◎　　　30 ♥

WHO YOU CALLIN' CHICKEN?

One week. That's all I had left.

Not even a full week. I had *five days.* Wait, no . . .

Four!

Because today was Monday, and the Hecklr show was scheduled for this Friday, which meant I had four days and nights to make sure the game was completely stable. I was in serious trouble.

Needless to say, Dad was right. A Hecklr show was being produced by a video game channel, but it wasn't a cable station. (That's Coach Bean for you: stuck in the eighties when it comes to pop culture. The 1880s.)

No, it was only ChickenHead LavaLamp, the crazy-popular YouTube channel with something like a bazillion followers and a gazillion-billion likes. Started by some fifteen-year-old kid in his parents' attic, the site has grown over the past two years to become the respected authority in all things gaming. The fact that ChickenHead LavaLamp even heard about Hecklr made my brain twitch a little.

But the idea that ChickenHead LavaLamp is going to be streaming a live game this Friday made my heart seize up with raw fear.

In fact, the very idea made my heart want to pack up and book a one-way trip to Antarctica.

I mean seriously—ChickenHead Lava-Lamp! When the channel's fifteen-year-old creator was trying to think up a name, he happened to see his parents' old lava lamp in their attic. And that lava was shaped like the head of a you-know-what. He had no idea that ChickenHead LavaLamp would become a multimillion-dollar empire in just two years. (Pretty sure if he knew, he would have picked a different name.)

The sad truth is, I can't run away from this. Sure, I could pull the whole game

GROSS, RIGHT?

down, but that would please exactly nobody. I could just let it run—bugs and all—but that would crush me more than anybody.

I'm proud of the game!

And then what if someday it came out that I was the game creator? What would Cyber-Girl think of me? Or more importantly—my dad? I couldn't deal with how disappointed he'd be.

All I could do was keep coding. And de-bugging.

For three days, I spent every spare moment coding. And de-bugging. And coding. And de-bugging.

Nick the Mimic tried his best to distract me. I'd be huddled over my phone, thumbs flying as I coded like crazy, and then I'd feel something. Eyes on me. I'd look up only to find Nick *staring* at me, eyes crossed, and his thumbs tapping on an imaginary cell phone. And then he'd start in with a robot voice:

"I. Am. Barth. Ol. Oh. Mew. I. Am. Only. Happy. Doing. *Math*. Problems. I. Am. Not. Human. Un. Plug. *Me*. Please."

Then I'd go back to coding. But of course, I'd have that stupid robot voice in my head for the next hour.

During those four desperate days, if I wasn't coding and de-bugging, I was walking somewhere. Like, to my next class. Or to the cafeteria. Or to the men's room. (But let me tell you, I was still thinking about coding and de-bugging . . . even in *there*.)

The problem was that whenever I decided to walk somewhere, Giselle would somehow, miraculously find me.

Every day brought a new collision, each one worse than the day before. And each time I found myself scrambling to make sure my phone didn't go flying through a window or under a herd of my classmates rushing to the next period. I was treated to a painful and embarrassing Giselle Body Check™ each day of the most frantic week of my life:

Monday: *boom!*

Tuesday: *ka-boom!*

Wednesday. *KA-BLAM!*

Thursday: [Insert your favorite Hollywood-style mega-explosion sound effect here.]

The only time I'm truly alone—with no threat of Nick making fun of me or Giselle barreling into me or Dad telling me to put away my electronic devices—is during lunch period.

Food? Hah, what is this food you speak of? These days, I eat nothing but symbols and numbers. I find the quietest corner of the cafeteria and continue coding in peace.

And that's where I was the day before ChickenHead LavaLamp was all set to stream a live game of Hecklr at Rancho Verdugo High. After four days of nonstop work, I was finally feeling good about the stability of the game. I might even be finished by dinnertime, which would certainly make Dad happy.

I was lost in a bit of code when suddenly the phone in my hands . . . disappeared.

What the hey?

I looked around in a panic, wondering what could have happened. Was I coding so hard that I caused the phone to disintegrate?

Then I heard a voice to my left.

"Just need to borrow it for a while."

I pinpointed the owner of that voice. Oh, no . . . it was Tigran the Tyrant! With my phone in his hands! And then he disappeared into the busy lunch crowd.

31 💎 31 🪙 31 ♥

ALL CODING AND NO FUN MAKE
BART A BORING BOY

I'm not proud of myself. But I kind of ... *snapped*.

Before snapping completely, however, I tried to get my phone back. The thing with Tigran is that you can never accuse him of stealing something. Because he's not exactly stealing. He's just borrowing it for a while.

I've seen it happen to other kids. If they're foolish enough to go to a teacher, then Tigran just shrugs and hands over whatever he's

175

"borrowed." The accuser ends up looking like an oversensitive jerk. It's stunning, really.

But this time I didn't care about looking like a jerk. I needed my phone! So I ran through the halls, looking for the top of Tigran's head among the sea of students. He couldn't have gotten that far.

"Mister Bean!"

I skidded to a loud, squeaky halt. *Mister Bean?* Was my dad around here somewhere?

"Over here, Bart."

I turned to face Mr. Lopez, who had his arms crossed and everything. Which meant he was *not* happy. Well, good. Because neither was I.

"Mr. Lopez, excellent! Look, I need your help."

"Bart, stop," he said, lifting a single hand, keeping his arms crossed. "You know the rules about running in the hallway. Do you know how dangerous that is?"

"But, Tigran—"

"I didn't see Tigran running. I saw *you* running. So, to slow you down, I'm giving you detention."

"*What?*"

Mr. Lopez blinked. I don't think he knew my voice could be that loud. But he recovered quickly enough. "Care to make it *two* days, Mr. Bean?"

No, Mr. Bean did not care to make it two days. One excruciating hour of after-school detention was more than enough. Every second that ticked by reminded me of all the coding I *wasn't* doing.

Staying *after school?* Dude, what did you do to end up here? Did you accidentally make the principal fall asleep? Are you here to make everybody in detention fall asleep? Wait . . . am I *already* asleep, and dreaming that you're in detention? And if you're here in my dream, will I *ever* wake up, because you're so crazy boring I might fall asleep inside *this* dream?"

I gritted my teeth and said nothing. I gritted my teeth so hard my entire body practically *hummed*. Because I knew that if I talked back, a teacher would pop out of nowhere and make me stay another hour.

The moment the late bell rang, I was out of my seat like a rocket, out the front doors, down to Rancho Verdugo Boulevard, racing all the way home, when, of course—

Ka-pow.

Giselle.

So, yeah, like I said. I kinda *snapped*.

But unlike most people my age, I didn't snap in the traditional sense—yelling, screaming, throwing a tantrum, hijacking a bus and ordering it to drive all the way to Hawaii, etc. No, my version of snapping is much more *subtle*—more *sublime*, one might say. (Don't worry; I had to look that word up, too.)

My version of "snapping" was hitting my laptop for an all-night coding session. But my mission now went beyond making Hecklr stable for its big debut on ChickenHead Lava-Lamp tomorrow.

No, I had a completely *different* update in mind.

32 💎　　　32 🪙　　　32 ❤️

THE BIG TO-DO

Yo yo yo! Live! From Rancho Verdugo! It's ChickenHead LavaLamp, y'all, streaming the game everybody wants to play . . . Hecklr!"

The kid with a microphone on the stage wasn't the creator of ChickenHead LavaLamp. (I think that kid is busy counting gold bullion in one of his Malibu estates.) Instead, he was one of the channel's online hosts, "Commander Magma," a YouTube star I've watched online for months now, and as much as I like to be all "whatever" about these kinds of things . . .

I had to admit: this was all *seriously cool*.

The high school athletic field—usually my dad's domain—had been transformed into a gamer's paradise. There was a stage in front of a fifty-foot jumbotron, where all the exciting Hecklr action would happen.

HEY RANCHOOOO VERDUUUUGOOOOO! ARE YOU READY TO GET LIT?

There were screens behind the bleachers, too, so the spectators could watch every pulse-pounding second of Lerkian-busting action, no matter where they were sitting. Plus, there were food trucks parked up and down the street, and college kids giving away free samples of snacks, and laser lights, and USB charging stations, and some DJ playing PC Music, and . . .

Oh, it was all so glorious.

"Up until now," Commander Magma said, "very few people on the planet Earth have been able to play this underground reality game called *HEEEEEECK-LUHRRRRRRRR!*"

The audience went *insane.*

"Unless you happened to live in Rancho Verdugo, or traveled here on vacation, you've totally missed out on one of the coolest games ever."

I'll admit it—my ego swelled up so fast that if I'd been wearing a baseball cap, it probably would have popped off the top of my head.

"So far, the elusive creator—or creators—behind Hecklr has remained in the shadows. But maybe this will inspire them to reveal themselves."

High up in the bleachers, I thought: *Uh, fat chance, dude.*

"Because tonight," Commander Magma continued, "for the first time ever, we're proud to present a live streaming game of Hecklr so you all can check it out for yourselves!"

Again, the audience went cray-cray. I went a little cray right along with them. Which I know is weird, cheering myself. But it would look weirder if I didn't shout and pump my fists, right?

Meanwhile, Dad was down on the field itself along with the rest of the Rancho Verdugo High School faculty. They had been pressed into service this evening to help keep the crowd—mostly high schoolers and middle schoolers—under control. The look on Dad's face was priceless. He understood exactly none of this, I'm sure. I could imagine him grousing. *Commander Magma? What the heck kind of name is that? And what's that awful racket coming from the DJ booth—is that an internet dial-up tone?*

"So, let's get this party started!" Commander Magma yelled, at which point the audience completely lost their minds. The faculty looked around, worried they might to have to stop a riot or zombie outbreak or something.

"Tonight's three players were chosen at random from the list of Hecklr registered players. Come on up to the stage. . . ."

The audience sucked in its collective breath in anticipation of the names being called. Imagine! To play a game live on ChickenHead LavaLamp!

"Giselle Blair!"

Wow, the Golem! Huh. Good for her.

"Nick Argento!"

Nick the Mimic, too? This is unbelievable. What are the chances?

"And finally . . . Tigran Sarkissian!"

Tigran the Tyrant? For reals?

No way, dude! How could it be possible that all three of my tormentors would be selected *totally and completely* at random?

Well, you probably guessed it by now, but last night I did a little work on the registered players list so that whenever ChickenHead LavaLamp's people—or anyone, for that matter—searched it for names, these three would pop up first. Always. No matter what.

Heh heh heh. This was going to be fun.

REVENGE . . . FROM SPACE!

I watched everything from the top row of a set of bleachers and wondered if Cyber-Girl03 was streaming this back at her apartment. I pulled out a pay-by-the-minute phone I bought earlier today (to replace the one Tigran "borrowed") and sent her a Slap-Talk.

BoringBart: Are you watching ChickenHead LavaLamp?

CyberGirl03: Yep. And the names of those

contestants sound awfully familiar. Is that Nick the same Nick who always picks on you? Nick the Mimic or whatever?

BoringBart: Huh, that's weird. I think you're right.

Nick "the Mimic" Argento was practically bouncing onstage, air-pumping his fists so hard that his wireless microphone headset almost slipped off. Weirdly, he proceeded to give his own introduction.

"Ladies and gents, introducing the reigning champ of Hecklr . . . the awesome . . . the amazing . . ."

"The humble," Commander Magma added.

"Hah hah!" Nick said. "Funny dude."

Nick was about to continue describing his all-around excellence when—*bam!*—he was accidentally-on-purpose body-checked by Giselle "the Golem" Blair. (I was still getting over the fact that she had an actual human last name.)

Nick squawked and pinwheeled his arms and almost went off the front of the stage—but recovered at the last minute. Giselle didn't seem to notice. Instead, she turned her attention to Commander Magma.

"Let's get this game going already!"

CyberGirl03: And isn't that the girl who always knocks you down? Giselle? There can't be more than one Giselle at your school.

BoringBart: You know, it could be. Hard to see from up here in the bleachers.

CyberGirl03: Well that's a weird coincidence, don't you think?

BoringBart: Our school's kind of small, I guess.

Commander Magma glanced over at Tigran, who looked as if he couldn't care less about being onstage. Or on the planet Earth, for that matter. "You ready, rock star?"

Tigran checked out his fingernails in response.

"Okay, Lerkian hunters, here's the deal," Commander Magma continued. "The giant screen is no ordinary display. It has been designed to respond to the alien attacks. If those little wiry suckers start winning and destroy the screen, molten hot lava will shoot out of little nozzles under the screen. The more you lose control, the more lava comes out of the screen."

Instantly, a disclaimer appeared on all the screens around the athletic field:

NOTE: "MOLTEN HOT LAVA" ACTUALLY ORGANIC FAIR-TRADE SHADE-GROWN GLUTEN-FREE ALLERGEN-FRIENDLY NON-STAINING ARTIFICIAL FRUIT JUICE KEPT AT AN AVERAGE TEMPERATURE OF A MILD AND PLEASANT 75 DEGREES.

CyberGirl03: It would be more fun if they used real lava.

BoringBart: Tell me about it.

"And just to make it interesting . . . if the Lerkians succeed in destroying the screen, then the entire athletic field will be sprayed with lava—and then covered in chicken feathers!"

CyberGirl03: What does that have to do with Hecklr?

BoringBart: I think that has more to do with ChickenHead LavaLamp's marketing department.

CyberGirl03: Lame. If I were the secret creator of the game, I'd be upset.

BoringBart: I don't know. I think it's kind of cool.

"Okay, players, put on your AR headsets, and I'll hand you the texting devices. Let's stop some Lerkians in their tracks!"

Now this was interesting. I had designed the game to be played on your phone, with the Lerkians visible only on a tiny screen. But with an augmented reality headset, everything around you was the screen. That must look seriously awesome!

Nick, Giselle, and Tigran put on their helmets, then turned to face the massive screen. The entire audience could see what they were seeing. Commander Magma pushed a texting device into each of their hands. When they typed their commands to the Lerkians, the words would appear on the screen for the rest of us to see.

Which is *exactly* what I was counting on.

"Ready . . . Set . . . Get your HECKLE on!" screamed Commander Magma. I'll bet he's been practicing that all week.

As if on cue, more Lerkians than I've ever seen wiggled their way onto the screen. All three players—even Tigran—took a step back in surprise. The audience gasped. There was a loud air-raid siren, and then bright-yellow sparks shot out of the massive screen. The Lerkians were on the attack!

34 ◆   34 ◯   34 ♥

THE LERKIAN EMPIRE STRIKES BACK!

Almost everybody in the audience was surprised by this new wave of Lerkians. They were absolutely ferocious!

In the normal phone version of the game, Lerkians do their destroying in a slow, methodical way. This gives the player plenty of time to shoo them away. But not these 2.0 Lerkians. They attacked the screen like they were wild dogs and the jumbotron was a giant pile of raw meat.

All of which was completely on purpose, of course. During my all-nighter of coding, I amped up the Lerkians' aggressive behavior to an extreme.

CyberGirl03: Is it me, or are these Lerkians extra mean?

BoringBart: Maybe it's just because they look bigger? You know, on a giant screen?

CyberGirl03: No, I'm watching this on my laptop and they're still scaring me.

BoringBart: Well, don't worry. There are three players fighting them all at once. I'm sure they'll be fine.

(Note: They will not be fine. I designed it that way. *Heh heh heh.*)

The Lerkians appeared to be quickly ripping apart the very fabric of the screen to reveal the chips and wires beneath. More sparks flew. Gotta hand it to the Chicken-Head LavaLamp physical effects team—it all looked really dangerous to be up there on that stage! The audience flinched and gasped with every sizzle and *pop.*

Nick said, "I've got this," then stepped forward, texting device in his hands.

Now what Nick typed was this: "Alien punks! Nick the Awesome is here. If I were you, I'd start running!" A typical opening gambit. Serious Hecklr players know to start with a general threat and save the big guns for later.

But on-screen, his command appeared like this:

GREETINGS, MY NEW ALIEN MASTERS! IF YOU SPARE ME, I'LL HELP YOU DEFEAT THE OTHER HUMANS!

The audience began to laugh and boo at the same time. Nick looked down at his texting device, then up at the screen, then back down to the texting device. He pulled off his headset.

"Wait, I didn't say that! What's going on?"

But it was kind of hard to hear him over all the *booooos*.

Giselle stepped in. And by "stepped in," I mean she stepped into Nick's space and knocked him over with the delicacy of a wrecking ball hitting the side of a one-hundred-year-old building.

"I'm not gonna let you double-cross us, jerk!" Giselle said.

And then she typed: "You'd better not let me catch any of you Lerkians. Because if I do, I'll use you to floss my teeth!"

But what appeared on-screen was a wee bit different:

I'M SO OBLIVIOUS TO EVERYTHING AROUND ME, I'M SURPRISED I HAVEN'T KNOCKED THE JUMBOTRON OVER YET.

The Lerkians, of course, ignored this weird moment of self-reflection from Giselle and continued destroying the giant jumbotron screen. I watched Giselle do a double take before she removed her own headset. Which was poor timing on her part, because that was the exact moment the Lerkians had done enough damage to trigger . . .

A gross, wet *lava burst!*
That nailed her right in the kisser.

Commander Magma told the audience, "Uh-oh . . . lava bursts *this* early in the round mean the Lerkians have a serious advantage." Then, to the players: "You'd better step up your game, people."

Nick, meanwhile, had climbed back to his feet and was furiously typing, trying to turn the tide. But he noticed that Tigran wasn't really doing much of anything.

"Yo, T! You going to play this game, or what?"

Tigran didn't bother typing anything on his texting device. But *somehow* his words began to appear on the screen anyway:

I BORROW STUFF FROM PEOPLE ALL THE TIME BUT NEVER RETURN THEM. HA HA HA, SUCKERS!!!

Now *that* got Tigran's attention. He ripped off his headset and looked at the screen with a defiant sneer. "Hey! I didn't say that!" A fresh round of jeers came out of the bleachers. I'm guessing these came from every student who had "loaned" Tigran something over the years.

Commander Magma cautioned him:

"Tigran, buddy, you might want to take this game more seriously. Because you're about to—"

Whoops, too late. A deluge of organic, allergen-free lava came out of a nozzle below the screen like water from a fire hose. Tigran was knocked off his feet. But that didn't prevent another text message appearing on the jumbotron screen:

OH, IF I EVER BORROWED ANYTHING FROM YOU, SEE ME AFTER THE GAME AND I'LL GIVE IT BACK.

When Tigran saw that, he didn't even bother getting up to resume the game. He *bolted*. And let me tell you, about a dozen or so middle schoolers stood up from the bleachers and went after him.

CyberGirl03: Are you watching this???

BoringBart: Crazy, huh?

Nick, meanwhile, was trying his best to gain some control over the on-screen Lerkians. But they were feasting on jumbotron parts like it was an all-you-can-eat buffet at Jo-Jo Ann's Giant TV Screen Emporium.

(Okay, so maybe that store doesn't exist. But if it did, I'd shop there all the time.)

"Please don't lava me, please don't lava me, please don't lava me," Nick mumbled, probably forgetting he was still wearing his headset and the *entire crowd could hear him*. Cue: waves of laughter. And then on-screen: a message from Nick that he didn't write.

GISELLE, YOU LOOK LIKE A GIANT RASPBERRY. HAH HAH HAH!!!

Nick's jaw dropped the moment he caught a glimpse of the screen. A very red (and dripping wet) Giselle followed his gaze up to the screen.

"I d-d-didn't wr-write that!" Nick stammered.

Which was true. This whole time, I had been the one writing their messages, in real time, right from my phone from my seat in the bleachers.

Now in all the time I've known Giselle, she's never made eye contact with anyone. Her MO was to slam into you and pretend like you didn't exist. At this moment, however, she locked eyes on Nick, and I swear, I could feel the heat from the fireballs of pure rage in her eye sockets from a hundred yards away.

Commander Magma could see it, too.

"Guys! Seriously! You don't want to fight each other. The Lerkians are going to win! And that means death by lava and chicken feathers for everyone in this field!"

YOU'D BETTER START RUNNING, NICH

Wait! I didn't type that—it must've come straight from Giselle!

Nick was no fool. He scrambled toward stage left, with Giselle the Heat-Seeking Missile close behind. Only he was a fraction of a second too late, because another air-raid siren blasted through the air. And then the biggest lava burst yet hit Nick and Giselle with the force of a tidal wave, knocking them clean off the stage and onto the grass.

This left poor Commander Magma alone on the stage. I sort of felt bad for him. He was hoping for a fun demonstration of Hecklr, but instead ended up refereeing a lava-soaked embarrassment that was being live-streamed to a million people.

And it was about to get worse.

"*Heh heh,*" Commander Magma laughed nervously. "Well, I suppose Nick, Giselle, and Tigran couldn't handle the pressure of planet-wide invasion. But unless we have some-one stop these Lerkians, all of you—yes *you,* in the audience—are going to know what it feels like to drown in lava, followed by a new suit of chicken feathers."

A few people in the crowd laughed ner-vously.

"No . . . um, I'm being serious. I have no way of shutting off this game. And unless someone steps forward to fight these things, we're all in for an incredibly messy evening."

I could see everyone on the field and in the bleachers murmuring to each other. *You go up there. No, you go up there. Are you nuts? I don't want to get sprayed by lava in front of a million gamers! We're going to get sprayed by lava, anyway!* And so on.

And I know I should have kept my head down, but I couldn't resist. Even though I went against everything I stood for (namely, staying seated, keeping my head down, attracting zero attention), I rose from my seat and shouted:

"*I'll do it!*"

BARTHOLO-WHO? PT. 2

WHAAAAAAAT was pretty much the reaction from the entire crowd as they turned to look at me up in the bleachers. Even my dad turned to look in my direction with shock on his face. *Is that my son? Speaking out loud? In public?*

Commander Magma ordered the tech crew to swing the spotlights in my direction. Everybody around me took a step back, leaving me brightly lit and completely exposed to the whole field. Gulp. What was I thinking?

My phone buzzed with an incoming message.

CyberGirl03: OMG. Is that YOU up there on the top bleacher? Did you just say that you'd play the game onstage?

BoringBart: Um . . . BRB.

"Well, come on down, bro!" Commander Magma bellowed from the stage, thrilled to have someone volunteering for this sure-to-be-suicidal mission. The whole joint might end up covered in fruit juice and feathers, but at least they'll have gone down swinging.

The rest of my body realized what my mouth had just done. I froze.

Commander Magma said, "Time is of the essence, dude. You don't want the Lerkians to win, do you?"

Well, it was too late to turn back now. So I started trotting down the bleachers, feeling a billion eyes on me. I could practically hear the questions rattling around their minds: *Who the heck is this guy? Does he even go to Rancho Verdugo Middle School?*

But by the time I reached the stage, one person recognized me. And that was Nick the Mimic, dripping wet with fake lava. And weirdly, he seemed genuinely happy to see me.

BARTHOLO-WOO-HOOOO!

"Hey, is that you, Bartholomew Bean? I didn't know you played!"

And as I ascended the stage, Nick had succeeded in getting a chant going. It was quiet at first, but within a few moments had reached fever pitch. The only problem is, they misheard Nick. So instead of the crowd chanting my actual name, this is what I heard:

MART! MART! MART! MART!

Up close, Commander Magma didn't seem as tall as I thought. He handed me an AR headset—Giselle's, I think—and tried to give me a texting device.

"No thanks," I said, showing him my pay-by-the-minute phone. "I brought my own."

"Go get 'em, Marty!" Commander Magma shouted. Then, under his breath, he whispered: "Because if you don't, I think I'm out of a job."

For a moment, under the heat of those lights and the shadow of the jumbotron, I felt crazy nervous. After all, I haven't really played the game since . . . well, since I was testing the beta version back at the beginning of the school year. Sure, I knew the game down to its tiniest scrap of code.

But what if I was no good at playing it?

The Lerkians resumed their destructive rampage. And looking at it through an AR headset . . . wow! It was more impressive than I realized. They were seriously determined to take out this jumbotron and turn the entire audience into sticky, feathered embarrassments. I didn't have much time left.

So I typed:

YOU UNDERESTIMATE ME, LERKIANS. I MAY APPEAR TO BE QUIET AND SHY, BUT I HAVE FRIGHTENED AWAY MILLIONS OF YOU.

Ooh, that gave them pause. A hush fell over the crowd.

What few people realize is that Hecklr is mostly a word game. Sure, you're supposed to go outside and track down these things. That's the physical part of the game I thought would impress my dad. But when you're squaring off against a Lerkian, it's not about how fast you can swing a bat or throw an inflated chunk of pigskin or kick a ball into a net guarded by some kid who looks like a psycho killer from a horror movie.

It's about creativity and confidence.

I had loads of the former, but as for the latter . . . well, that's something I really needed to work on. So essentially, I faked it.

I HIDE AMONG THESE ORDINARY BEINGS. THIS IS MY DISGUISE. BUT I WAS SENT HERE TO PROTECT THIS PLANET FROM THE LIKES OF YOU.

The Lerkians, it seemed, were calling my bluff. They ramped up their attacks, digging deep into the guts of the jumbotron. Behind me, I could see the hiss of nozzles and maybe even the rumble of giant bags containing millions of chicken feathers. This was going south, quickly. CyberGirl03 was watching. My *dad* was watching. I had do *something*.

Namely: I had to cheat.

LOOK. THE CHEAT CODE IS A TIME-HONORED GAMER TRADITION, BUILT FOR PLAY-TESTING PURPOSES. I SHOULD BE ALLOWED TO... UH, PLAY-TEST A STUNNING VICTORY!

On the jumbotron, these words appeared:

I CAN BANISH YOU WITH A SINGLE GESTURE, LERKIANS.

But on my pay-by-the-minute phone, I entered in the secret code that would cause all Lerkians, everywhere in the game system, to suddenly disappear for an hour.

Then I made a tiny bye-bye wave.

And then the Lerkians . . .

. . . *went bye-bye.*

Every last one of them vanished from the screen.

Throughout the field, there was complete, utter silence. What the heck just happened? Even Commander Magma looked confused. Did this boring kid from the bleachers just win the game?

Nick finally broke the silence. He looked up at me from below the stage, blinking.

"Dude."

THE BILL BEAN FACTOR, PT. 3

And then, of course, the crowd went wild when they realized they weren't about to be covered in cold sticky lava and billions of chicken feathers—which were probably not organic, unless there

were currently entire farms of naked chickens out there.

Commander Magma, realizing he wasn't about to be fired from his YouTube gig, was overjoyed. "Dude, what is your name? Marty? Hardie?"

"Uh, Bartholomew Bean?" I said, glancing at the screens all around the field. My own dumb face stared back at me. The cameras had found me, and gone in for an extreme close-up. Yikes.

"Marty, man, how did you do that? You banished the entire Lerkian fleet with just a wave of your hand!"

"Practice?"

"How long have you been playing Hecklr?"

"Er, ever since it was available for download."

"You discovered some kind of cool, next-level backdoor code, didn't you? Come on, you can tell us, the millions of people streaming

ChickenHead LavaLamp right now. It'll stay between us, I promise!"

"Um . . ."

"If you had a message for the secret creator of Hecklr, what would it be?"

"Keep up the good work?"

"Do you think he'll someday create versions of the game for other cities besides Rancho Verdugo?"

"Maybe?"

Commander Magma put his arm around me. "Marty, my main brain man, you play it close to the chest. I like that. And congrats on kicking serious Lerkian butt. But hey, Chicken Heads, don't go anywhere. We've got loads of Hecklr walk-through videos streaming on our site right this very second . . ."

After what felt like an eternity, I finally climbed down from the stage. Nick the Mimic was all over me like we were long-lost war buddies or something. "Dude! That was wild! Can you show me how you did that?"

Giselle, meanwhile, stared at me with her big cow eyes. She didn't know how I'd defeated the Lerkians, but she also knew she didn't like it. On the plus side, she was a.) making actual eye contact, and b.) not pummeling into me like a steamroller.

Tigran? Who knows where he was. Maybe he was still running from the angry mob of kids who had "loaned" him things.

Before Nick could drag me away to teach him my secret tricks, I felt a tap on my shoulder. I spun around to face. . .

Gulp. My dad. Coach Bill Bean, who had the most curious expression on his face. As if he couldn't

figure out if he should be angry, or confused, or proud, or maybe a combination of all three.

"Interesting game," Dad said, gesturing with his head toward the stage. "I thought you didn't play."

"Honestly, I don't," I replied, which was sort of kind of the real truth. I didn't play the game so much as code the game. "I may have checked it out once or twice to see what the fuss was about."

"I'm still not sure what you did to win the game."

"Beginner's luck?"

"What's that in your hand?"

I looked down. He meant the cheapo pay-by-the-minute phone I'd bought earlier today. Uh-oh. Busted.

"A friend of mine borrowed my phone yesterday, and, um, I forgot to get it back."

"So you bought another phone?"

Double busted! Oh so cleverly, I tried to

change the subject. "So, what did you think of the game? Kind of cool, right?"

Dad sighed. "I'll be honest, I still don't understand what was going on. What was the stuff with the lava and the chicken feathers? Is that part of the game?"

"No, not really. And they were kind of playing it wrong. It's about teamwork, really—"

"And the players insulting each other?"

"Uh, that wasn't part of it, either. Hecklr is *really* about—"

"Were those kids up there friends of yours?"

"I wouldn't exactly call them friends."

"Good. Because they really embarrassed themselve. I'd hate to be in their shoes walking around school tomorrow."

Now I was about to tell my dad: *Seriously, don't worry about them. They're all jerks!* But then I thought about Nick, cheering me on like a loon. I thought about the hurt look in Giselle's eyes. And I even felt bad about Tigran, who might still be running through the streets of Rancho Verdugo.

"C'mon, buddy," Dad said, squeezing my shoulder. "Let's stop off at Frosty's before heading home. I'm sure Pickleback will appreciate the treat."

Once again, my dad was offering me one of my favorite treats on the planet. And once again, I was pretty sure it would taste sour.

As we walked, however, my cheap pay-by-the-minute phone buzzed. I thought it might be SlapTalk, but instead it was a message from the Hecklr servers. It was an anonymous post from a player:

```
I know who you are. And I know
what you did tonight.
```

Whoa . . . *what?*

37 ♦   37 ⬭   37 ♥

BART MARTY BEAN TRIUMPHANT!

I woke up on Monday to discover I was the toast of the town.

And I don't even like toast!

But seriously—as I walked up to the front doors of school it seemed like everybody recognized me.

"Marty, you *rocked* the game last night."

"Can you teach me that wave good-bye thing?"

"Dude, Marty, that was so *lit*."

Yeah, okay, so most of my fellow students thought I was "Marty Bean," the nobody from nowhere who stepped up and single-handedly beat the Lerkians. So I guess in a way I was still anonymous.

And then Nick himself came walking up to me, hand in the air, expecting me to return a high five. Like . . . what?

"Bartholomew! Don't leave me hanging."

So, yeah, I gave him a high five. I was too confused to do anything else.

"I've been thinking about this," he said, walking with me toward our next class as if we were BFFs who did this every day. "I think the Hecklr people released a 2.0 version on the night of the ChickenHead Lava-Lamp event just to mess with us. So all the old strategies didn't work. But somehow you knew. And that's crazy impressive, man. You gotta teach me some of your moves."

The more he talked about the game, the more I realized: whoa, Nick the Mimic may actually want to be friends with me.

After my first class, naturally, I ran into Giselle in the hallway.

But here's the crazy thing: she didn't run into me at all.

In fact, she went out of her way to *avoid me*, keeping her eyes on me the whole time, as if I were a banana peel on the high school track. I couldn't believe it. So I did the only thing that made sense.

"Giselle!"

She froze mid-step and turned her head cautiously in my direction. "Hey, Bartholomew."

She knew my name. Like, my *real* name. What?

I didn't know what to say. So I stammered out the first thing that came to mind:

"Um, I think the Hecklr people released a 2.0 version on the night of the ChickenHead LavaLamp event just to mess with us. So all of the old strategies didn't work."

Giselle stared at me for another second or two, then said "Thanks," and continued down the hall.

Whoa.

The rest of my day was full of random classmates shouting out "Hey, Marty!" and "You schooled the Lerkians, bro!" And then came lunch period.

Now, normally, I'm sitting alone in the cafeteria, coding like crazy. But on this day, I found myself surrounded by people who wanted to hear all about my Hecklr strategies. I'll admit it: I kind of loved the attention.

But then I felt this presence behind me. The air itself seemed to thicken with unease. Everyone at the table had the same worried expression on their faces as they looked behind me. I turned, bracing for the worst . . .

And indeed, the worst was standing there. Tigran the Tyrant.

"I know what you did, and it's not cool," he said, then held out my beloved smartphone. I took it, warily, wondering if he was going to snatch it back and yell "Psych!" But instead he simply turned away and started to disappear into the lunchtime crowds.

As overjoyed as I was to have my phone back, I excused myself from the table and went running after Tigran. I caught up with him near the pizza and fries station. My hand reached out and grabbed his arm.

"You were the one who sent me that anonymous message, weren't you?" I asked.

Tigran looked down and grimaced as if my hand were covered with fish guts and mayonnaise. I quickly removed it from his arm.

"I didn't send you any message," he said.

"But you just said—*I know what you did.*"

"Yeah. I saw all that coding stuff on your phone. I figured you were the one behind the whole thing."

"You . . . um . . . oh."

Suddenly, my blood was about as cold as the soft-serve at Frosty's. What was Tigran going to do, now that he knew the truth?

"You didn't have to be a jerk about it and embarrass me in front of the entire school district," he continued. "You could have just asked for your phone back."

"But why did you take it in the first place?"

Tigran just shrugged. As if to say, *Bees sting. Dogs bark. The moon spins around the Earth. I borrow stuff.*

"Anyway, cool game."

And with that . . . Tigran was gone.

I was relieved for about 2.5 seconds. Because if Tigran didn't send that anonymous message last night, who did?

On my walk home from school I navigated my way around the high fives and "Yo, Marty dude, you're awesome!" comments and wondered who could have figured out my secret.

By the time I reached the apartment complex, though, it hit me like a fifty-foot jumbotron screen.

CyberGirl03 was on her balcony, as usual. She waved at me, but this time I didn't wave back. Instead I went up to the front door of her apartment and—gulp—*knocked*.

38 ◆   38 ◎   38 ♥

THE GIRL BEHIND THE HANDLE

I wasn't sure if she would answer. Heck, I wasn't sure if I should even be knocking. This was already a day where my life had basically turned upside-down. And now I might be making things even crazier.

But slowly, the door opened. I expected to see CyberGirl03 standing there, but instead she was sitting down. Like, in a wheelchair.

"Hi, Boring Bart."

"Hi, CyberGirl. I got your message."

"What message?"

But she said it with a sly smile that told me I had been right. *I know who you are. And I know what you did tonight.* That, however, didn't explain the mystery of why the best friend I've never met was trolling me.

"Do you want to come in for a snack or juice or something?"

"Sure."

I followed her into the apartment, which was just like ours—only reversed, like a mirror image. Some part of me wondered if the promise of a snack and juice would lead to . . . blackmail! You know, where she makes me promise to fork over half of the profits of Hecklr in exchange for her silence about me creating it.

But a.) there were no profits, since I always intended the game to be free, and b.) that just didn't seem like the CyberGirl I knew.

"My mom's still at work—she won't be home for another couple of hours," CyberGirl told me as she rolled to the fridge and opened the door. "Apple? Peach? Sweet tea?"

"Whatever you're having. Uh, can I ask a possibly stupid question?"

She paused to look up at me. "Depends on how stupid."

"Hah-hah," I replied, which may have been the fakest, most nervous laugh ever. "Why don't you go to Rancho Verdugo? There are ramps and stuff for people with disabilities." Then, seeing the nervous expression on her face, I quickly added, "See, I warned you it was probably stupid."

"No," she said. "Not stupid at all. I ask myself the same thing. And I wish I could. But . . . let's put it this way. It's a miracle I'm even talking to you in person. Normally strangers freak me out. Crowds *especially* freak me out. So I do school at home. You know, cyberschool? Through my computer?"

"You're probably comfortable around me because I'm so boring."

"You're not boring at all, Boring Bart. You might be the most interesting person I know."

Were my cheeks red? Possibly. But it was probably the sweet tea, which has been known to increase the flow of blood to the face . . . okay, I'm totally making that up.

"So why did you send that anony-mous message to the game last night?"

CyberGirl grinned. "*Ah-hah!* Busted! So you do admit it! You're the secret creator behind Hecklr, aren't you? You're the one who sent it to me in the first place. I should have known all along."

"Maybe . . ."

Stop it, cheeks! I could feel them getting even redder. *Ugh.*

"Well, whoever created the game should know something. I didn't finish the mes-sage. It should have read: *I know who you are. And I know what you did tonight. And I want to thank you.*"

"Thank me? I mean, thank him? For what?"

"Hecklr actually makes me want to go outside, which is something I haven't wanted to do since, like, fourth grade. So I wanted to thank you for that. Or thank *whoever* created it."

"I'll pass that on," I said, "if I see whoever created it."

At this point, if you cracked a raw egg over my cheek, you'd have had a sunny-side up in a matter of seconds.

"My name is Aaliyah, by the way."

"Um, and I'm Bartholomew."

"Yeah," Aaliyah, a.k.a. CyberGirl03, said. "I know. Maybe you can show me a little coding? I've always wanted to try."

THE BILL BEAN FACTOR:
THE FINAL CHAPTER

When you're flying high, that's the exact moment you should buckle your seat belt, pull out the airline sick bag, and double check that there's an inflatable life vest is under your seat. Because things could go south at any given moment.

That moment came when I keyed into my apartment and noticed that Pickleback hadn't come bounding up to lick my face and try to knock me to the ground. That wasn't good.

I cautiously walked down the hallway to my room. Pickleback was on my bed, looking vaguely guilty about something. *I tried to stop him, Bart, I really did, but . . . well, he's kind of my master.*

That master, a.k.a. Coach Bean, a.k.a. my dad, was sitting at my desk, looking at my computer. On the screen were the coding guts of Hecklr. Oh, no. *Triple* busted! After all these months of working in the shadows and keeping my work on the game a total secret, three people in the last three hours have figured out my secret identity. First Tigran. Then CyberGirl03/Aaliyah. And now . . . my Luddite dad.

Ugh. This must be a new world record. I would make the world's lousiest superhero or secret agent.

"I don't know what I'm looking at exactly," Dad said, "but I have a feeling it isn't your math homework."

What could I say? I didn't want to lie to my dad anymore.

"No, it's not my math homework."

"Now I know I'm just a knuckle-dragging gym teacher, but that was computer coding on your screen, wasn't it?"

"Don't sell yourself short, Dad! Your

knuckles don't drag on the ground at all . . ."

"Bart."

"Yes?"

"You created that insult alien game, didn't you?"

"Yeah, I did."

Dad sighed. "Buddy, I have to say . . . I'm really disappointed. If you created that game, that means you were making fun of those three kids last night."

"But you don't understand. They're the three jerks who always pick on me! I didn't mean to take it that far, but . . ."

My words trailed off, because I knew I could only finish that sentence with the truth. *"I thought that if I took my revenge, I'd feel a little better about myself."*

"Bart, you have a brilliant mind. It's scary how smart you are sometimes, because I don't know anything about this stuff. I'm a gum-chewing high school gym teacher who somehow was blessed with the brainiest kid on the planet."

"Clearly I'm not that smart. You figured it out."

Dad blinked. "Um . . ."

"I didn't mean it that way!"

"Anyway, considering how brilliant you are, it's very important to learn that you can't use those gifts to hurt people."

Now it was Pickleback's turn to sigh. Wonderful. Even *he* was ashamed of me.

"I thought it would feel good," I said, "totally humiliating them in front of the whole school district."

"And did it?"

"No," I said, truthfully. "Not at all. I think one of them, Nick—you know, the humble kid—even thought we were friends. Which makes me feel like a crumb."

"The one who was chanting 'Mart, Mart, Mart'?"

"I think he was saying *Bart*."

"Sounded like 'Mart' to me. I had a lot of people ask me about 'Marty Bean' today, and if we happened to be related. Anyway, I guess there's only one thing left for us to discuss."

Oh no. Here it comes. The moment I was dreading.

I had the distinct feeling that I was about to be taken off all electronic devices for the foreseeable future. And I could foresee a long, long, *long* future. As in, I wouldn't be allowed to have so much as a pocket calculator until my senior year of high school.

Goodbye laptop, so long cell phone, sayonara SlapTalk. No more coding for me. Wi-Fi signals would be mere legend and rumor, and someday I'd tell my grandkids about the magic time when I was allowed to access some mythical place called "The Internet."

I gritted my teeth and awaited punish-
ment.

DAD VS. ALIENS

Explain this game to me. How do you play?"
Stunned, I un-gritted my teeth. This couldn't be for real, could it? Was Dad actually asking me about Hecklr? Even Pickleback cocked his head slightly, ears up, wondering if they were deceiving him.

"Are you serious, Dad?"

"Of course. I wish you would have showed it to me earlier."

This boggled my mind. *Dad . . .dude . . . I've only been trying to get you to play since the beginning of the school year!* But I quickly recovered.

"We'll have to go outside for the full effect. I really don't keep many Lerkians around here. They're kind of a distraction."

"Lerkie-whats? You mean the dental floss monsters?"

"Come on, follow me."

As Dad, Pickleback, and I walked outside and headed down to Rancho Verdugo Boulevard, I explained the basics to him. Which was kind of like trying to explain second-year algebra to a caveman, but whatever. I was impressed he kept up with me at all.

"Now, point my phone at the neon sign and look through my screen."

We stood in front of Joey G's Back to the 50's Diner—a Lerkian favorite. Dad pointed the phone at the sign and his whole body jolted.

"Whoa! It's one of those alien things from the game last n—no, wait, there are two of them. Three!"

"Yeah, they really like this place. Must be the grease."

"So, what do I do now?"

"Tap the screen to get their attention, and then—"

"Wait! They're ripping apart the neon sign!"

"Yeah, that's what they do, Dad. Now once you get their attention, you type in something to threaten them."

Slowly but surely, my dad understood the game. Threats, he could do, even though at first he was typing lame things like:

I'M GOING TO CALL THE POLICE

and

IF YOU DON'T COME DOWN FROM THERE I'M GOING TO MAKE YOU DROP AND GIVE ME 20.

Coach Bean, man. He's a gym teacher down to his very soul.

Even Pickleback got into the act, barking at the neon sign because his human family members were shouting and laughing and pointing. Pedestrians who strolled by probably thought we were goofy in the head. But that was fine. We were having too much fun.

But I forgot something important. In all the excitement of last night, I forgot to dial back the Lerkian aggression factor. Soon we had dozens of the little jerks crawling all over Joey G's neon sign, as well as nearby traffic lights and cars. Dad kept looking through my phone and freaking out.

"There's another one! And whoa . . . another one! They're everywhere!"

"Let me see."

Dad was right. Rancho Verdugo Boulevard was positively SWARMING with Lerkians. At this rate, they'd tear about the entire Boulevard (well, at least the virtual version I'd programmed into the game) in no time.

"This is not good," I said.

"So, what do we do?" Dad asked, genuine panic creeping into his voice. Which was surprising and kind of flattering.

"We ask for help."

I stood up on a chair outside Joey G's place, cleared my throat, and did something very unlike me (again). I shouted to everyone within earshot.

"Hecklr players! If you've got your phone with you, we could really use your help."

There was an awkward silence for a moment. I thought, *Great, now I'm the one who's going to look like a complete fool. And in front of my dad, too!*

But then some high school kid, maybe sixteen or seventeen, recognized me. "Hey, aren't you that Marty Bean guy, from the game last night?"

"Yeah!"

The kid smiled, then started shouting out to everyone else. "We got a serious Lerkian situation, bros. Marty Bean is leading the charge!"

Ugh. "Marty" again. But whatever.

On the plus side, within seconds, everybody who had downloaded the game was pulling out their phone. Soon at least two dozen people were spread all up and down Rancho Verdugo Boulevard, shooing away Lerkians as fast as they could find them. This drove Pickleback bonkers, by the way. I felt kind of bad; maybe I could design a special add-on for dogs and their human companions.

Dad was impressed. "So this is kind of like a team sport?"

"Yep," I replied. "Exactly like a team sport. With, uh, cell phones."

Which, okay, let me just say:

Finally!

"That's pretty cool," Dad said.

It was amazing. There was hope for Coach Bill Bean yet.

EPILOGUE

HECKLR 2:
THIS TIME, IT'S PERSONAL

So I'm standing in front of the class, and I've just started giving the most important report of my life. I'm nervous, because a *massive* part of my future depends on this.

I'm about three sentences in when I realize: *Houston, we have a problem!* I look up from my paper and quickly scan the classroom.

"Er, as I was saying . . ."

You know how you look out into the class and hope for a bit of encouragement to keep you going?

"Ummm . . ."

But there's nothing. No reaction whatsoever.

That's because *everyone in the classroom is a LERKIAN!*

Actually, I wasn't standing in front of a classroom. I was sitting in front of my laptop, doing some coding. The screen was full of letters, numbers, and symbols. But I could practically see the little alien jerks on my screen. And they weren't happy about being bossed around.

Aaliyah—formerly known as "Cyber-Girl03"—was with me, too. Over the past few weeks we'd been exploring good ol' Rancho Verdugo, looking for new locations for possible Lerkian infestations. She's pretty good at spotting them, I must say. (Then again, she's lived here a lot longer than I have.)

Together we've been working on system improvements for the entire game. And you know who's been a really great play tester? Our buddy Nick—you know, the guy formerly known as "Nick the Mimic." He still doesn't know that I designed Hecklr, but he's always happy when I tell him there's been a new update, and he's always (and I mean *always*) eager to tell me what he thinks. It's pretty great feedback.

Dad's eased up about me and "screen time" and "electronic devices" and all that. And you know, I've eased up on my zero-tolerance policy concerning tossing a ball around outside in the punishing, crushing, life-withering heat of Rancho Verdugo. It's kind of fun, actually. And sometimes, Aaliyah joins us.

All of which is great, because I'm hard at work on a new project. Improvements to the game are fine, but I'm thinking bigger. Bolder.

I'm thinking about taking Hecklr national. That's right: coast to coast.

And maybe even someday we go international!

That's right, Lerkian Empire. Wait until you see what I have in store for Hecklr version 2.0 . . .

To be continued in. . .

UNBELIEVABLY
BORING
BARTHOLOMEW
GOES
HAWAIIAN!*

(*Note: probably not the real title of the next book. But Bart insisted. What can we say? The kid has Hawaii on the brain.)

ABOUT THE AUTHORS

JAMES PATTERSON received the Literarian Award for Outstanding Service to the American Literary Community from the National Book Foundation. He holds the Guinness World Record for the most #1 *New York Times* bestsellers, including *Middle School, I Funny,* and *Jacky Ha-Ha,* and his books have sold more than 380 million copies worldwide. A tireless champion of the power of books and reading, Patterson created a children's book imprint, JIMMY Patterson, whose mission is simple: "We want every kid who finishes a JIMMY Book to say, 'PLEASE GIVE ME ANOTHER BOOK.'" He has donated more than one million books to students and soldiers and funds over four hundred Teacher Education Scholarships at twenty-four colleges and universities. He has also donated millions of dollars to independent bookstores and school libraries. Patterson invests proceeds from the sales of JIMMY Patterson Books in pro-reading initiatives.

DUANE SWIERCZYNSKI is the Edgar-nominated and Anthony Award–winning author of *Canary* and *Revolver.* He's also written for comic books, TV, and film.